JHUMUR PANDAY

DECEIT BROUGHT US TO ASSAM

AND OTHER STORIES FROM THE BARAK VALLEY

Edited by
Debjani Sengupta

THORNBIRD
NIYOGI BOOKS

Published by
NIYOGI BOOKS
Block D, Building No. 77,
Okhla Industrial Area, Phase-I,
New Delhi-110 020, INDIA
Tel: 011-26818960, +91 7428978881
Email: niyogibooks@gmail.com
Website: www.niyogibooksindia.com

Editor: Shirsha Ghosh & Vishikha Deogawnka
Design: Nadeem Ahmed
Cover design: Pinaki De
ISBN: 978-81-990243-7-3

Publication: 2025

Printed at Niyogi Offset Pvt. Ltd., New Delhi, India

CONTENTS

Foreword	5
Introduction	9
Deceit Brought Us to Assam	17
Saluk Flowers Have Bloomed	28
Sandhyamani, Anchu Bura And…	42
The Boy	53
The Witch	57
Enceinte Woodlands	69
Sisirkona Will Play On	79
Oozing	83
Troubled Tales	93
Phoolbasiya Buri Goes Back	100
There Goes Srimati	111
Upstream	123
Glossary	136
Editor's Acknowledgement	142

FOREWORD

Owing to the many reorientations of the boundary of Assam and the migrations to the state in the colonial and postcolonial periods, Bengali today is one of the largest linguistic groups in Assam. The Bengalis are concentrated more densely in the Barak Valley of Assam comprising three districts: Cachar, Karimganj and Hailakandi. How deeply Bengali language and culture has now spread its root in the valley can be easily seen in the martyrdom of 11 young souls on 19 May 1961 for safeguarding the interest of the Bengali language.

It needs to be mentioned that dislocation and displacement, often voluntary and mostly under duress, and the resulting human crisis are inseparable parts of the history of the Bengali community in the Barak Valley. One of the largest displacements took place after the referendum of the Sylhet district on 6 and 7 July 1947. The probity of the manner in which the referendum was conducted was questioned and the scar remained fresh in the heart of the displaced.

However, the pang of being uprooted and the crisis of identity rarely became thematic concerns in the Bengali literature of Assam for the first two decades following the Partition. The landless and destitute people were so engaged in earning their livelihood, and so recent and close was the experience of being uprooted that they failed to distance themselves from their immediate context and explore the themes in literary productions.

Before that, the marginalised Bengali culture and literature of the Barak and Surma Valleys had their thriving centre in Sylhet or Srihatta. After the Partition, this lifeline was destroyed. The displaced populace of the erstwhile East Pakistan had to establish a new epicentre for the creative output of the Bengalis. Bijit Bhattacharjee, editor of the Hailakandi-based magazine, titled *Sahitya*, called it 'Ishan Bangla', meaning the space comprising the Barak Valley. As mentioned earlier, for many years, the struggle of the people of this space was not properly represented in the literature of the valley. Nature and modernist emphasis on the individual remained their staple food.

It was with the launch of the *Atandra* poetry movement of the 1960s, centring around the eponymous little magazine, that things started changing. The poets of this movement for the first time focused on the broader exploration of themes like identity, language and social justice. Similarly, in 1969, a powerful short story movement in the Barak Valley manifested itself through the little magazine called *Anish*, founded by Shyamalendu Chakraborty, arguably the pioneer of short story writing in the valley. *Anish* was followed by another significant little magazine, called *Shatakratu*, spearheaded by Tapodhir Bhattacharjee, which became the indispensable mouthpiece of the young and socially conscious short story writers. Since then, short story as a genre found firm footing in the literature of the Barak Valley.

Some of the then young writers who emerged mostly through these two magazines are Mithilesh Bhattacharjee, Ranavir Purkayastha, Arijit Choudhury, Badarujjaman Choudhury, Malay Kanti Dey, Sekhar Das, Swapna Bhattacharya, Dipendu Das, Amitabha Dev Choudhury, Tirthankar Chanda, Soumitra Baishya and others. Many of them are senior professionals now and continue to write wonderful stories. Bijoya Deb, Subrata Kumar Ray, Param Bhattacharjee, Rahul Das, Sharmila Datta, Himasish Bhattacharjee and Jhumur Panday appeared in the next phase, maintaining the strong tradition of short story writing in the Barak Valley.

Many of the stories from the Barak Valley delve into the search for identity and belonging within the diverse cultural landscape. They examine the relationship between the valley's inhabitants and their surrounding geography, including the hills, rivers, tea gardens and the neighbouring states. Some of the stories explore the complexities of human relationships, including love, family dynamics, and the challenges of navigating social norms. Also, the Barak Valley's unique geographical features, such as the Barail Range and the Barak River, often serve as a backdrop for the stories, influencing character and plot development. And finally, the Valley's history of diverse ethnicities and cultures are reflected in the stories, highlighting the richness and complexity of the region's identity.

Nirmal Kanti Bhattacharjee

INTRODUCTION

The Barak river valley is a distinct geographical region in the state of Assam (India) with a strong literary and cultural identity of its own that can be seen as autonomous from the larger forcefield of Assamese literature and language for varied historical reasons. The geographical spread of the Barak river valley covers three districts of Assam (Cachar, Hailakandi and Karimganj), the Jatinga Valley of North Cachar, the Jiri Frontier Tract (Jiribam) of Manipur, Kailashnagar–Dharmanagar area of Tripura and four districts of present-day Bangladesh: Sadar Sylhet, Maulavibazar, Habiganj and Sunamganj. The three districts of Assam and the four districts of Bangladesh have emerged out of the two districts of Cachar and Sylhet in the British colonial period, together known as the Surma Valley division, since the districts became a part of Assam in 1874. In 1947, after the Sylhet Referendum, a major part of the Sylhet district (leaving only Karimganj to India) was transferred to East Pakistan. Hence, the remaining Indian portion of the valley is called the Barak valley today. The inhabitants of this region speak Sylheti, Bangla, Meitei and other tribal languages like Dimasa and Rongmei-Naga. In the tea gardens of the region, the language spoken by the tea garden labourers, known as *baganiya bhasa*, is a mixture of Bhojpuri, Bangla, Assamese and Prakrit words of ancient origins.

In Assam, the landless Muslim peasants had emigrated from erstwhile East Bengal as far back as 1901, while British-run tea gardens had brought in workers from Bihar, Uttar Pradesh and elsewhere, often under duress. After the Partition, Hindu middle class refugees were joined by other tribal exiles from the Chittagong Hill Tracts and from Mymensingh and Rangpur, who crossed into Assam for a variety of reasons. The resultant tension between native population and the 'intruders' often took the form of linguistic and economic clashes, sometimes between the same religious or ethnic groups. Apart from the agriculturists and artisans who came as refugees to the Barak valley, there were a large section of Sylheti middle-class economic migrants to the region who were not 'refugees' in the sense meant in Partition studies. Their identity had been formed not as a result of rivalry against Muslims but in opposition to the Assamese Hindus who had resented their elite status and government jobs that many had enjoyed from British times. The Bengali settlers claimed that the Barak valley in lower Assam had always been an important cultural centre of Bangla. Sylhet had been a centre of politics, education and cultural activity from medieval times with notable Sanskrit scholars residing in the region. In the fourteenth century, with the conquest of Hazrat Shah Jalal, Persian and Arabic learning expanded in the region. During the Chaitanya period (end of fifteenth and till the beginning of seventeenth century) the expansion of Bengali language and literature took place in the neighbouring regions of the Surma-Barak valley, in Jaintia, and the Dimasa and Tripura kingdoms, particularly under royal patronages. Barak valley had given birth to poets like Golam Hossain and Krishna Chandra Narayana, a king in the Cachar region who composed devotional poetry. In the modern age, poets and writers like Ashokbijoy Raha, Nirmalendu Chaudhury, Hemango Biswas, Khaled Chaudhury and Syed Mujtaba Ali, were all born in the valley and the region had a flourishing culture of little magazines and literary journals that were often the result of individual efforts and little state funding. Thus towards the end of the 1950s, with the rapid promotion of Assamese as the state language, the Bangla speakers of the Barak valley began to feel worried. The subsequent *bongal kheda andolan* to drive out Bengalis from the Brahmaputra valley alarmed the Bangla speaking minorities and when the Assam Official Language Bill was passed in 1960 restricting the use of their mother tongue, the Bengali population was filled with disquiet.[1] On 19 May 1961, a procession of students and writers went on a peaceful march through Silchar town demanding recognition for Bangla as a medium of instruction in schools and colleges. The police fired on the unarmed demonstrators and a 15-year-old student, Kamala Bhattacharya and 10 others died to become 'language martyrs.'

Barak Valley's chequered linguistic and social history is the background to Jhumur Panday's writings. Her stories are multivocal in that she uses different registers of the Bangla language for different characters that may be read as an attempt to carve out a dispersed political and linguistic space that is the Barak valley today. Another aspect that sets her stories apart is that the narratives that are collected and translated in this volume mainly deal with the migrant tea garden labourers. These writings highlight the plight of the workers recruited on indentured contracts from British times and their successors. As historian Jayeeta Sharma notes: 'Well after Indian Independence, tea's migrant workers remained a permanent labouring class, marked by a history of racialization and displacement.'[2]

---

[1] Arupjyoti Saikia, *The Quest for Modern Assam: A History: 1942-2000* (Gurugram: Penguin Random House India Private Limited, 2023), 251-253.

[2] Jayeeta Sharma, "'Lazy' Natives, Coolie Labour, and the Assam Tea Industry," *Modern Asian Studies* 43, no. 6 (November 2009): 1287-1324.

Jhumur Panday's stories enable her readers to enter a complex world of oppression, racialization and labour. They construct the elaborate linguistic and labouring practices within the agro-industrial enterprise of tea manufacturing that has continued in Assam from British times. The systematic pauperization and oppression of tea garden labourers therefore forms an important subject of Panday's stories and the harsh working conditions of the workers even in contemporary times, are used to assess the ways in which the state has reneged on its promise to ameliorate their conditions. These stories, often from the point of view of the workers themselves, indict political parties who, irrespective of ideology, come to power to sustain old practices of exploitation and semi-feudal methods to subjugate the ostensibly free workers.

The particular geography and history of the region has given Barak valley writers a different political trajectory than their counterparts in West Bengal, especially in their ceaseless efforts to preserve their language. Given the geographical distance from the literary metropolis of the mainland and their minority status in the hierarchical chain of Bangla language publishers and the publishing industry, this effort is both laudatory and filled with uncertainty. This has also resulted in a concerted search for a form that would encapsulate and represent the experiences of instability and exile that is a dominant feature of short fiction of this region.[3] In Panday's oeuvre, the short story is foregrounded because that format is an expression of the region's ambivalence not only to mainland Bengali literary culture but an articulation of the region's location in terms of the Indian nation. Her stories explore homelessness, identity and belonging and carve out a different aesthetic impulse from 'mainstream' canonical Bangla fiction of the 'mainland' both in theme and language. Thus the specificities of region and politics have enabled this corpus of writing to be substantially unique. Jhumur Panday is a remarkable writer who needs to reach a wider audience. She understands the connections between gender, livelihood, labour and land; therefore her stories are shot with a subtle political flavour that is both unmistakable and potent. I hope these translations will win her a serious band of readers both at home and abroad.

Debjani Sengupta

[3] Bijit Kumar Bhattacharya, in his *Uttor Purbo Bharotey Bangla Sahityo* 1:9, coins the writings from the Barak Valley as comprising the third sphere of Bangla literature, separate from those that are produced in West Bengal and Bangladesh. This has drawn howls of protest from mainly West Bengal critics who see Bangla literature as a pan-regional phenomenon without specificity of region, politics and identity.

DECEIT BROUGHT US TO ASSAM

On his cot in the courtyard, Chargola Exodus sat with his legs dangling. Then, he stretched out. The clear sky was adorned with stars. Uncountable, really. Bhojon *buro* used to ask a riddle: 'A plate full of betel nuts, even the seller cannot count. What is it?' Chargola had pondered what that could be.

Really, the sky decked with stars resembled a plate full of betel nuts. Chargola smiled to himself. A sweet fragrance filled the air. What flower could it be? *Kamini*? It could be, since there was a *kamini* tree in the backyard. How the name of the flower evoked a lingering sense of pain in the corners of his heart!

'*Khaye le, Dada*. Please eat.'

'I will eat here.'

'The night is almost gone, eat up.'

A while ago he did hear the nine o'clock chimes from the tea estate. Purna used to ring the bell earlier. Now, it was perhaps his son Sashi who rang the bell.

Mongri brought out a steel plate full of rice with pulses cooked with greens and crab chutney. Exodus started to eat.

'Where did you find crabs?'

'Caught them in the brook near the fields.'

Chargola continued to eat sitting on his cot. The beautiful ambience of the star-lit sky and the fragrance of *kamini* made him relish his meal all the more. His grandmother too had made chutney with garlic and dried chilies.

'Will you take some more?'

'What?'

'Rice.'

'No, I am full.'

Exodus, having eaten to his heart's content, swallowed his burp. When he was young, he used to work in Mekle Saheb's bungalow. Saheb despised his habit of burping. One night he was almost thrown out of the house in the pitch darkness of *amabashya* because he had burped out too loud!

Ramcharan's mother was away at that time to the hillock of Shonmari, to offer puja. After a day's hunting in the forest, Saheb had brought home a deer. Exodus had been tagging along with him all the while. The animal was carved, skinned and cooked well by Sudhanyo *kaka*. *Kaka* at that time was the Saheb's head cook. After the hefty meal of deer meat, Exodus had presented himself burping before the Saheb. And the Saheb...

'Won't you wash your hands?' Mongri asked while clearing away the plates.

'Yes. Right away.'

Exodus looked at the star-laden sky once more and inhaled the fragrance of *kamini* with all his heart. *Aha re*, Kamini was unmarried then. Her dusky body was filled with a thousand charms. Once, while returning from *karamer dal*, she had slipped at the foothills. On the night of the *jagran*, she had danced with everyone.

In the village they asked us to go to Assam
They promised us tea seated on the floor
But what we got was a spade to dig
What we got was to pluck the leaves
Oh! You cruel fellow Shyam!
Deceit brought us to Assam…

She had looked sideways at Exodus to sing:

You got our names down in the register
Imposter Shyam,
Deceit brought us to Assam

Exodus had been dancing too that day. He had gulped down two-three glasses of *hadiya* brew. He remembered everything…

Under the dense canopy of *sirish* trees
Amidst the tea plants, with tender care
We do back-breaking work
Oh Sirish!
How many people know our story?

'Where are you off to?'

'Didn't I tell you about the *jagran*?'

'You did?'

'Hmm...'

'Maybe...go.'

Exodus had grown forgetful. He was almost four score and seven or eight years old. He was born in the year 1921 during the Mulki agitation. The purpose of the rebellion was to escape to their own country, the *muluk*, hence the name: Mulki agitation. However, the Sahebs called it the Chargola Exodus because it was from the Chargola Estate that the labourers first began to leave. Nobody knew who had named him Chargola Exodus.

He once again stared at the sky. He could see one or two clouds had come floating by, hand in hand. The moon peeped out from behind them.

'Hey Ramdhani.'

'What?'

Ramdhani had looked up while skinning the bamboo. The sight of the chowkidar made the colour drain away from his face.

'Let's go to the bungalow.'

'But why?'

Ramdhani's wife had just brewed tea for him. She had come out shivering.

'You will get to know there. Come.'

'Have your tea before you go', Ramdhani's wife had said.

'Keep your tea', the chowkidar had said.

The meaning of a summon to the bungalow was well-known to Ramdhani's wife, Swarnalata. Swarnalata's eyes were already red from blowing into her kitchen fire. Now, despair and anxiety made the tears roll down her cheeks. The baby too was kicking inside her womb; the boy who would one day be called Exodus.

When Ramdhani was brought back to the courtyard, the young healthy man of twenty-two was a living corpse. Oh yes, he had committed a terrible crime! He had passed by the Saheb's bungalow while galloping on a horse, one of Bharat Saheb's horses that his father had looked after. Ramdhani was bed-ridden for days. However, Chowkidar Ravan, while escorting him, had warned him, 'Keep a tree bark tied to your backside.'

Under the incessantly lashing whip, did Dutta Babu's hand quiver at least once? But it was a Saheb doctor who had healed him with medicines. Everyone knew how good the doctor was.

His grandmother had recounted all that to Exodus. His mother, Swarnalata, had died after giving birth to him…

The white-washed clouds were dispersing hand-in-hand. The sky was glowing with a smiling moon. The fragrance of *kamini* came wafting to his nose.

'What are you doing?'

'Can't you see I am gathering flowers?'

True, Kamini was gathering *seuli* flowers as she hummed a song.

'And after this? *Ki korbis*? What will you do?'

'I will gather some ripe jackfruit seeds that Ma will roast in a sand-filled *kadai*.'

'What else will you do?'

'I will cleanse the house with white mud.'

'What else?'

'I will play.'

'What else after that?'

'Don't you bother me…'

The girl had stood there, wide eyed.

An owl was hooting somewhere. A snowy owl. Sleep would not come. Mongri would also come at daybreak.

A distant sound of *madol* echoed all over. While inhaling the perfume of the *kamini* that filled his heart, Exodus tossed on his bed.

Tea leaves are plucked in galore
But when weighed in the machine
Nine *mon* of leaves become six
That pains our hearts
Oh Saheb, do hear
Kaala Pani is what we cannot bear…

Want to go to your muluk? Your country? Somebody's whisper could be heard in the wind. Fear, panic, happiness had filled their bodies and hearts. From one estate to another, a single line had been transfused: 'Will you go to your *muluk*?' Actually, at its inception, it was the Swadeshi workers like Deosaran Tripathi and Gangadoyal Dixit who had infused the idea of *muluk* into people's minds. The oppressed and tortured tea garden labourers had responded to that with fervour. They had seen a new light of hope. At that time, almost everyone wove a common dream of escaping back to their own land. Brinda had even composed a song…

Let's go away to our *muluk*, my friend
No more shall we pluck leaves

No more shall we bear our master's kicks
Oh friend! No more the burden of slavery!

After a bit of tossing and turning, Exodus sat up. He watched a shooting star go past in the sky. The faint memories of his grandparents were resurfacing again. It was common knowledge that Deosaran Tripathi was arrested because he was involved in the non-cooperation movement. Imprisoned first at Sylhet and then at Jorhat jail, he had died after a hunger strike of 45 days.

And what had happened to Gangadoyal Dixit? Who knew! Whenever *kaka* spoke about them, his hands automatically folded together in reverence.

And his mother, Swarnalata...Oh! What did she look like? Even now, Exodus's heart ached when he thought of his dead mother. He visualised her face to invoke sleep. After all, carrying Exodus in her womb, Ma had begun her journey for *muluk* and with many others had boarded the train from Karimganj station. The Swadeshi crowd had funded to make the women and children go first. But the trains did not move. The labourers had to start picketing at the station. At last, the railways had to succumb to their demands. The men had to walk till the Chandpur river port.

A choir of crows woke Exodus up. The moon's glow had illuminated the bushes and the trees; perhaps the crows had mistaken it for daybreak? When would Mongri come home? Mongri was his great grandson, his granddaughter Samali's child. Cawing, the crows now seemed to be flying about. Exodus gaped at the sky once again. Did Swarnalata, with Exodus in her belly, reach her *muluk*? While boarding the steamer from Chandpur port, pierced with the white men's bullets, Swarnalata had fought for her life till she gave birth to Exodus. His father, Ramdhani, along with many other labourers, succumbed to the bullets as well. The River Padma had turned red that day with the blood of the tea workers. Brinda had strung together a song too on that:

In my tears,
My man got washed away
In Padma's water
Oh my friend
My man faced the bullets
He is washed away, that's what I heard,
My friend
In Padma's water…

'Father, did you not sleep yet? *Ghumali nai*?'

The door opened and the boy came out.

'No. Mongri has gone to the *jagran*.

They will return. Your grandson has gone too.'

The son and the grandson, everyone acted as a sidekick to the MLA nowadays. Previously, it was *kaka* who used to perform this duty; that too only during the elections. Elections used to be lucrative affairs. With a healthy supply of blankets, sheets, food and drinks, everyone would pose as an emperor. Nowadays people followed the leaders all through the year. The grandson got 5000 a month from the minister. Who worked a strenuous job nowadays? Oh, the boy satisfied so many of his cravings with that money! What if he had to act like a tame dog? Exodus heaved a sigh. What blame could be put on them? Born during the times of bombings, he too had to do the slavery of those who had killed his parents. His throat was parched. Oh, there was the water that Mongri had kept aside in a steel glass. Exodus gulped the water in one go. He gazed at the sky again and at the bushes and trees. He listened intently to the faint sound of the *madol*.

Sardar says work!
Babu says bring them here,
Saheb says I will skin you alive
You, deceiver Shyam, you duped us to Assam

Why was his throat parched again? Hadn't he drunk a considerable amount of water just now? Sudhanya's rooster was crowing. Dawn was near. One by one, the birds would start chirping. The crows had been cawing all night. How beautiful the moon looked! The morning star was also glistening. Bhojon *bura* used to show them to him and name them: *Kaalpurush, Saat Bon Kritika*, the ones that were planets, the ones that were stars…so many things Bhojon *bura* had taught him. Once again, the faint sounds of the drums came to Exodus's ears. It was now being played on a faster rhythm. Was Mongri dancing? Of course, that was it. Exodus loved Mongri dearly. He even got him admitted to the school but nothing good came of it. Exodus got off his cot. He inhaled the *kamini* once again deep into his heart. The chirping of the birds had filled the air. Dawn was breaking over the trees.

The moon and stars had vanished, one by one. Exodus crossed the courtyard and the road and stood alone by the wide world. It was flooded with the silken light of dawn. The pain of dying ripped through Exodus. He visualised his mother Swarnalata's face and listened to the lapping of the Padma. He could hear the steamer as well. His hands had become numb. The pain that cleaved through his body was the pain of being born, of dying. It played through his mind and body as Exodus began his long trek towards the Chandpur River port…

Translated by Aishwarya Banerjee and Debjani Sengupta

SALUK FLOWERS HAVE BLOOMED

ONE

Saluk flowers are in bloom
In the deep waters
Oh! Bring them to me
My beloved Shyam

Carrying a vessel of water on her hip and a pot on her head, Ashtami came laughing all the way.

'Why are you so merry? What's there to laugh about?' Giving a momentary break to sweeping the yard, Khepli *buri* stood upright. The tiny bun on her head had come undone.

'I am not laughing, *Didi*. Please sing the song again.'

Tying her tiny bun, Khepli *buri* began her song:

Saluk flowers have bloomed...

Ashtami laughed again.

'*Khub joyanki utheche lai*? Your youth is blooming too much, isn't it?'

Ashtami laughed again.

Khepli *buri* swore with an expletive, '*Bhatarkhagi*!'

'What did you say? Do you have a lover?' While crossing the courtyard, Ashtami turned around with the pot of water still on her head.

'Your youthful vigour has made you proud, I see. You know what? I was young too, once. When I stepped out on the streets, at least ten men ogled at me.'

'Yes, I know. No wonder you were pregnant with the Saheb's child.'

'What did you say? How dare you!' Khepli *buri* chased her with the broom in her hand.

Preparing herself for a fight, Ashtami first slid down the pot from her hip and then from her head. 'And your sister? Do you think we don't know about her scandals? Everyone knows.'

'What scandal?'

'She lived with her father-in-law.'

'So what if she did?'

'You want to hit me? Go ahead. Do it. I warn you, if you dare touch my water, you have to pay for it!'

'If you dare cross my courtyard again, see what happens!'

'Don't you dare come to our backyard to forage for saag!'

'You dare me?'

Polu came out as a mediator and quietened down Khepli *buri*.

'What is going on here, *Pishi*? And Ashtami, why are you egging on an old person? Go home.'

This side-show had already attracted a crowd of people by now. While loading the pot of water on her head, Ashtami focused on Polu. 'Why is it bothering you? Your wife procured a job by being a sycophant to the minsters. My God! How proud she has become!'

Seeing Polu nonchalant, she says again, 'What is the status of my *Pishi*'s ID card?'

Polu didn't speak a word. Public demands had to be heard. Even their curses were to be borne. One couldn't answer back! Every insult had to be digested and it was only then that one could hold on, earn a bit extra. His father, Sumanta Bakti, had passed his lifetime wearing threadbare clothes. He had lost his life to police bullets while demanding a bonus, still clad in those rags. His mother too had spent her life like that. Sometimes she had dug for wild potatoes and sometimes had plucked edible leaves to feed herself and her children. What a pity! How honest they were! Times had changed. But the change was nothing that his father had dreamt of! Polu understood that but what could he do?

That was why he now indulged in sycophancy and in opportunism to procure a meal, sometimes even a chicken-meal! He had a TV at home; he had even arranged a eighth-class pass certificate for his primary-educated wife and had helped her get recruited in the *anganwadi*. His children too went to school. The same school where Polu himself was the president. Who could imagine that! The same Polu who could hardly sign his name. Moreover, the panchayat vote was drawing near. What if he became a candidate for the post of the president this time!

It did not happen in the last election in spite of all his efforts. How quickly Sadananda's name had slipped off the minister's tongue! Polu was asked to contest for a membership. But he had not. After all the effort, the candidature of a mere member was not worth it.

Khepli *buri* now kept aside her broom to sit, with her legs stretched out, under the guava tree. The assembled crowd, unable to partake of any more fun from the quarrel, eventually dispersed. Oh no! Half of the courtyard still remained to be swept.

Today at dawn, Khepli *buri* had dreamt of Poran's father and after so long, a melody had come up to her throat; that unfortunate hussy had ruined everything! Khepli *buri* tried to invoke that melody yet again: *Saluk* flowers have bloomed…

'*Pishi*?' Polu squatted beside her. 'Make a cup of hot tea, *Pishi*.'

'Really, that audacious girl ruined my mood early in the morning.'

'Forget it, *Pishi*. Why don't you make some tea? This time the winter is long.'

'That's true. I shiver constantly through the night.'

Buri made a glass of *mola* tea; they were called that as the leaves were hand-crushed. She often entered the tea factory to steal some leaves. Then she either crushed them or cut them to dry under the sun. The sardar never barred Khepli *buri* from taking a few leaves. What would he have said! There was a time when *buri* used to pluck a *pon* of leaves. The praise of her skills and her beauty had spread far and wide. And wasn't that why Boro Saheb…

'This jamun tree of yours appears new, is it, *Pishi*?' Polu said while sipping his tea.

'Yes, I think this year it will bear fruit.'

'The fig tree has also grown.'

'Yes, the fruits are also one of the sweetest you will ever have. Will you eat a few? '

'Not now.'

'Then have some *muri*.'

'Yes, you can give me some.'

But the puffed rice had gone a bit soggy. After serving Polu, she too sat with a glass of tea and some *muri*.

'What happened to my house to be built under *Indira Awaas*?'

'Don't worry! It will happen.'

'When? It has been days, I tell you...'

'It will happen this year only. Let the minister come.'

'Shukla, Mithila, everyone has got theirs, but in my case...'

'You got your BPL card, didn't you? Don't worry, you will get everything. Oh, now I remember, there will be a blanket distribution tomorrow. You must go.'

'Where?'

At the club. Eleven o'clock. If you come late, you will not get one. Come at the earliest.'

After finishing his tea, Polu went off. Khepli *buri* resumed sweeping and her singing as well.

Saluk flowers have bloomed
In the deep waters...

TWO

The dusk had faded. Stars blossomed one by one. With her blurry eyes, she witnessed all the shining and shooting of the stars at the heart of the fuzzy sky. She had already gathered a pile of dried leaves by sweeping all morning. She had even gathered some dry twigs from here and there. Now she made a fire at one corner of her clean courtyard to warm herself. She did this often during the winters. And the warmth of the fire enticed her neighbours: Fuchan's father, Sumitra's mother, Prakash's wife and many others. Even the children were drawn towards the fire but Khepli *buri* stopped them from coming near.

However, nobody appeared that day. The fire had been burning for long. Standing and waiting for Polu's blanket distribution all morning had caused her body to ache. Swarms of people had been waiting too but nobody had showed up with the blankets. Some said the minister would come to distribute the blankets himself. Perhaps that was the delay. Khepli *buri* had thought that if she got to meet the minister, she would entreat him for her *Indira Awaas* house. He was after all the minister. But after a long while, she had to return home. On her way back, she had bought one *powa* flour from Sanchit's shop and now she ate a roti with her tea.

Polu was a big-time liar. The entire day had gone in vain. If she had gone to the woods instead, she could have foraged for some *babubhaji*, banana flower or *kochusaag*. Khepli *buri* poked the fire with a long stick. Her father, Lokkhindor, used to build such a fire! So many people used to throng their courtyard during the winter evenings to warm themselves. And Khepli used to thrust beans and potatoes into the fire to roast. Oh, how wonderful the smoked beans and potatoes used to taste! Ma would catch some *gorui* from the streams with hooks and she would make a gravy with radish. What delightful taste that fish gravy had! During the winters, Gohur *bura* used to dole out jaggery in the middle of the field. In order to get some, Khepli used to run with her bamboo *fara*.

Her father often made her tea with machine-cut leaves. What an intoxicating smell surrounded that place! How many myriads of tastes did her tongue have then! The air carried so many fragrances! Where were those tastes gone now? Where were those smells? Where were her mother and her father? Where was Gohur *bura*? Nobody existed anymore. Nobody was left. Not even her son! He had gone to Punjab with Boro Babu's daughter but never returned. She had heard that he now worked in a factory. And what about his wife and children? Nobody knew! Let him be. Wherever they were, they had her blessings.

Mumbling to herself, *buri* closed her eyelids. A deep sigh was stuck in her throat. She poked the fire again and firmly tied up her open hair. Poran's father has been appearing in her dreams since the last two days and her heart was heavy. The song had come unbidden to her throat: *Saluk* flowers have bloomed...While singing this song at *karam*'s *jagran* that she had with Poran's father...she stirred the fire again. What terrible things people had said about her!

The fire was going out but there was no sign of anyone. Without people, without some gossip, what was the point of the fire's warmth?

'Hey, why didn't you go to take the blanket?'

'Blanket?'

'Yes, they have just finished distributing.'

'Finished? And I stood there all morning!'

'They have just finished and have left.'

'Didn't the minister come?'

'No.'

That is why nobody had come around the fire.

'Did you bring one for me?'

'Yes. Here it is.'

'Was Polu there?'

'Yes, he was. He had to be.'

'He didn't even tell me. Wait, let him seek votes this time. Let's see who goes around with him, campaigning!'

'Listen, *Didi*. I just heard that this time the president's seat is reserved for women only.'

'Women?'

'Yes, and if that happens, you must stand for election. Everyone is considering you.'

As they stood talking, Ashtami's sister, Nabami passed by flaunting her blanket. Khepli *buri* stirred the fire once again. She who roamed the woods for leaves and vegetables, if she could sit on the president's chair! She whose hair was matted! All these thoughts floated into her head like a dream. The bird was singing: *Daughters, rise! Women, rise*!

Poran's father's memories made Khepli *buri* hum again: *Saluk* flowers have bloomed...

THREE

Early in the morning, Khepli *buri* was sweeping her courtyard. Leaves from the guava trees and many others were strewn all over the courtyard. The guava tree had grown huge within a year and now covered the entire courtyard. It bore fruit all year round. The tree with its flowers, leaves, ripe and unripe guavas, lit up the little courtyard. Below her veranda, two white and purple Indian periwinkle flower shrubs bloomed and at the corner of the courtyard, one gardenia tree. During the month of *Chaitra*, the fragrance of the flowers intoxicated the world!

And during moonlit nights, their beauty was immeasurable. On the left of the courtyard, there were other trees like a *harsingar* and a land lotus. There were two chilli and brinjal plants as well that bore fruit through the year. A moringa tree had stood in another corner. When the flowers had bloomed, birds came flocking to its branches. Its leaves could heal pain. But the other day, the tree just came down. Perhaps...

'Hey, *Pishi*.'

Khepli *buri* stood up, putting aside the broom in her hand.

'Where were you when you were distributing blankets, Son? Now you are here calling me!'

'I have kept a blanket aside for you. Now you will be the one distributing them! *Indira Awaas* will also happen at your words.' Polu laughs his heart out.

Buri stared blankly at Polu, with the broom in her hand.

'We will make you the panchayat president this time.'

'Me?'

'Whether you become or I, it's the same thing!'

'Nabami said something about it. But am I literate enough?'

'So what? Many illiterates have become ministers and MPs.' Polu sat down under the guava tree.

Buri kept aside her broom to sit beside him. She took a dollop of lime out from the small amount tucked away at her waist and started to knead it on her palm.

'Ashtami has given me a blanket.'

'Ashtami? What about the ferocious fight you two had that day?'

'Forget it. Young blood!'

'Listen! Ashtami too wants to stand as a candidate. But I said clearly that if the seat is reserved for a woman, then Khepli *Pishi* will be the candidate.'

'Did they agree?'

'Let the minister come. Subhash is the one instigating Ashtami. But I am there for you, *Pishi*, aren't I?'

Now, she got up and crushed the lime between her lips. A squirrel dropped a half-eaten guava right near *buri*'s lap. The yellow oriole lurking behind the tree called out.

'I heard that the minister had beaten Sanat Thakur after pulling him off his car.'

'Hmm.'

'Why did he beat him? They belong to the same party.'

'He must have been doing something wrong, why else?'

Polu's mobile started to ring. After walking about and talking over his phone, he sat down again. But *buri* did not.

'You seem worried. Don't you worry. I will manage everything. The 108 bus now ferries patients on the highway. Don't you see many improvements? The 108 bus, mid-day meals at school, BPL card, old-age pensions, all-round primary education, I have even given Nabami the job of a cook in the school. And don't forget, many people are enrolled in ASHA. Roads are getting repaired; so many projects and so much progress, money is in the air, you just have to catch it. Every project means frauds amounting to lakhs of rupees. It's all about the business of stealing. Our father's generation is long gone.'

Buri's eyes begin to bulge.

'Yes. A hundred crore rupees got eaten up in the name of progress.'

Buri's eyes further enlarged.

'Do you know why am I saying all this to you? Because you too will have to say all these except for the last few sentences. I must go now. A lot of work is pending.'

'Would you like some tea?'

'I just had tea at Subhash's shop.'

Polu left. *Buri* sat again under the guava tree with a palm against her cheek, pondering about progress, mid-day meals, the 108 bus. The yellow bird sang out again from behind the leaves. A squirrel was hopping around the branches of the guava tree. Forgetting everything, *buri* sang aloud again, '*Saluk* flowers have bloomed...'

FOUR

Dawn was breaking. Some were on their way to graze their cattle. '*Hyat*, *hyat*,' their cries reached Khepli *buri*'s ears. The soft light was peeping into her room through the slits of her bamboo hut and window. The light lit up her face as well.

Embracing the soft light, *buri* tossed on her bed. The guava tree spreading its branches through the courtyard was like a guardian to her little hut. *Buri* could hear the murmuring of the leaves, the chirping birds on its branches. Khepli *buri* would contest the election. Polu, along with everyone, considered her win to be imminent. But she had heard that the manager's wife was going to contest for the same post.

Wasn't it ludicrous that Khepli *buri*, with matted hair and a wrinkled face was going to compete against the *Memsaheb*!

So many projects and so much progress, money in the air—one just had to catch it! ASHA, mid-day meals, old-age pension…which one to leave, which one to keep, who knew? Polu said so. And did Polu know or understand everything? And if his father, Sumanta Bakti, talked once in a while through his tongue, there wasn't much one could do. That was why he had to bear the minister's cuss words, had to hear cuss words from the public. The birds were chirping again; the leaves were murmuring. Let everything be. Vote, progress…a smile appeared at the corner of *buri*'s lips. Her wrinkled face looked like a freshly bloomed lotus.

Poran's father had appeared again in her dreams last night. Her heart was heaving, just like the red *saluk* flowers. Turning on her jute-quilted bed, *buri* hummed once again to her heart's content as she traversed along the banks of the lotus pond, passed the mossy hill, towards the large water-body radiant with *saluk*…

Translated by Aishwarya Banerjee and Debjani Sengupta

SANDHYAMANI, ANCHU BURA AND...

ONE

'Anchu Anchu
Kadi badamchu
Anchu Anchu'

'Don't you dare! Wait till I catch you! I shall certainly go and tell your father! I have never seen such a cheeky girl. Such audacity!' Anchu *bura*, livid with anger, cleaned his utensils.

However, Sandhyamani could not be stopped from needling him with her jeering, 'Anchu Anchu.' Sandhyamani had woven her call around Anchu and why wouldn't she? Anchu was the owner of about seven to eight jackfruit trees that yielded many fruits. Anchu didn't sell them and the fruits lay there, decaying. From time to time, neighbours collected them. That day *bura* was not home and Sandhyamani had picked up a jackfruit only to find herself face to face with him.

'You stole my jackfruit?'

'Stealing? So many people are taking them but you call me a thief! Take your jackfruit, *le, le.* It's just a bit far, otherwise Ramavatar's place has a huge tree. The fruits are all falling off too.'

'Then go to his place. Go!'

'Yes, I will. Who cares about your jackfruits?' Sandhyamani began to leave, throwing the jackfruit at him, but she turned around at the call of *bura*.

'When you have plucked it off the tree, take it.'

'Sandhyamani will take your jackfruit? Go feed it to the worms.'

Anchu *bura* barked out in English, 'Stop it!'

He was once a chef at Alekh Saheb's bungalow and he often spoke English words. Something that Anchu *bura* was very proud of!

'Don't you flaunt your English. My brother could jabber in English too. Understand?'

'Why wouldn't he? He was the illegitimate son of the Saheb. Haven't you noticed his fair skin?'

'How dare you? Say it again. Come on, say it.'

Just a few days back, Sandhyamani was catching crabs from the small stream in front of Anchu *bura*'s hut.

'What are you up to?'

'Can't you see? I am catching crabs.'

'Give me a couple. I will make some chutney out of it.' The thought of garlic and dried chilli paste mixed with crab meat conjured up saliva in *bura*'s mouth.

'Haven't even caught one. And you are asking me to give you two!'

'Then you can't catch them here.'

'Why not? Is this your father's property?'

'Don't you dare!'

Just then a crab had pinched Sandhyamani's hand.

It was because of this relationship Sandhyamani shared with Anchu *bura* that she had woven her song around him. The mountain-top in the west was gradually turning orange as the sun set and a flock of colourful birds were returning to their nests. Anchu *bura* fumed with anger as he washed the utensils vigorously. Meanwhile, Sandhyamani, her gaze fixed on the vast expanse of the sky, the ombre mountain-top, and the flurry of birds, gave forth a sing-song call:

'Anchu Anchu
Kadi Badamchu…'

TWO

Sandhyamani was filling water from the mountain stream. Through the *helencha* bushes, a frog peeped out while a *titir* bird, just a little distance away, pecked on the ground. Amidst this tranquil scene, a *dahuk* called out seductively.

Anchu's brusque question shattered the calm, as he set down his pot to fill water. 'How long does it take you to fill water?'

'Don't you have any other time? *Hami ailei toro ashbar mone porey?* I just arrived and now you remember to come here? You have all the time in the world, but I have to cook for my father before I leave for school. *Baap khayek jabey kamey.* Father will eat and go to work...'

'Don't talk so much. Your vessel is full.'

While throwing some water out from the overflowing pot, Sandhyamani said, '*Bura* just can't wait. What do you have to do back home? No children or grandchildren either! Don't you have to kill time all day?'

Holding her pot at her waist Sandhyamani walked with the grace of a *birangona*. The *dahuk* called out again...

Looking away, Anchu muttered to himself loud enough to be heard, 'Just come to play in the evening, I will show you.'

THREE

The yellow black-headed oriole had been incessantly calling out since the morning, *ishti kutum, ishti kutum...* Sandhyamani, humming to herself, was giving a mud plaster to the floor. Last night, she had revelled at *karam*'s *jagran*. The lyrics of the *jhumur* songs were floating in her mind. At the courtyard, she caught sight of the yellow bird perched on the jamun tree. Mother used to say that the call of the *ishti kutum* presaged the arrival of a guest but Sandhyamani saw none. After her mother's death, her uncle cut all ties with them. One aunt had died of malaria last monsoon. And she had no one from her father's side. Aghor *bura* had raised her father. He used to manually feed leaves to the machines in the tea estate. Those were the days before electricity, but *bura* was long gone…

Her younger brothers came in with a couple of *chaltas*, unripe green fruits. 'Give us some rice.'

'Can't you see I am cleaning the house?'

'We are leaving then.'

'Where are you off to? You didn't eat since morning, nor did you go to work. What are you doing all day? Staring at the idol in the *nachghar*?'

'Idol? It is still wrapped in straw. There is hullabaloo at the Battala.' The two boys ran away.

Sandhyamani forgot the lyrics she was humming. Her heart felt heavy. The bird had flown away too. At the tender age of nine, she was burdened with a family to care for. How tiring it was sometimes, physically and mentally! Apart from all that work, clutching her torn books, she went to Jagat master's school. But some days, after the household chores, she could not attend. Her mother had died just after the birth of the youngest boy.

The fig tree her mother had planted still bore fruit. One couldn't finish eating the sweet fruits. So many birds thronged its branches to eat the figs—*bulbuli, fultusi*, parrots and the tailor bird. So many of them. Her two brothers showed no inclination to study, so their father had found them a job at the tea garden. Oh my God! She could hear the sound of bullets. Is her father alright? Sandhyamani had seen her father and some others picket to demand a hike in the *Pujo* bonus. Every year, like a ritual, some chaos reigned about the bonus just before *Pujo*. Last year, Pocha had died at a similar meeting. This time? Even her brothers had gone. Without bothering to shut the door, Sandhyamani ran out with mud-stained hands...

FOUR

On his earthen hearth, Anchu *bura* was cooking catfish. He had caught it that morning from Bhatipokhra using his fishing spear. The delicious smell wafted over the hut. However, his cooking was nothing like his mother's. Her culinary skills were amazing. Alekh Saheb had relished her delectable pork and lamb dishes. Even the venison that he had hunted! The cold almirah would be filled with all kinds of meat. What times they were: the English era!

Oh, the flames had gone out. The logs outside were sodden from yesterday's rain. Anchu had set out for Battala to sell some *dheki* saag yesterday when the rains came down heavily. What could he do on his own? His wife had left him long back, a few days after their marriage and she would now be an old woman with silver tresses. Anchu *bura* had crossed eighty many moons ago. He was uncertain of his age; he was eighty-five or eight, but he looked no older than sixty. It was rumoured that his wife had remarried at Dholai Bagan, but did Anchu lay his eyes on her again?

The plaintive cry of the *ishti kutum* echoed once again from the jackfruit tree. Where are his *kutum*, his kin? There was no one, nowhere. Who would visit me? Don't cry so, silly bird! He brought out the iron *phunkni* to stir and blow the fire. The dying fire glowed again with vigour. This *phunkni* was brought to the house from the *chaghar* by his father after requesting Gohur Mistri. That was another story.

The smell of the fish curry came wafting to his nose. Anchu, sitting with outstretched legs, crushed tobacco on his palm. The fire was going out again. Anchu stirred it once more. He washed the rice and put it to boil. He liked the rice only when it was cooked in boiling water and drained well. While cooking, Ma used to recite Khana's proverbs. Where did she learn all those?

The amount you give rice
The water should be thrice
When it shall overflow, stir the rice...

What was the next line? Sudden forgetfulness gripped Anchu these days. He tried to remember but couldn't. Oh no! What commotion was that? He took off the rice pot from the fire and walked out, crushing tobacco in his palm.

FIVE

As the dusk yielded to a night of impenetrable darkness, one wondered if it was the night of the new moon, for the heavens themselves were bereft of a single star. Sandhyamani, flanked by her two siblings, took refuge upon a thin gunny sack, with an earthen lamp casting a meek glimmer beside the hearth.

'We are hungry. Give us something to eat.'

Sandhyamani took a deep breath. A long deep breath.

'Our father is alive, isn't he, *Didi*?'

'I don't know. I don't know anything.'

'I found him sleeping in a pool of blood.'

'Father has been taken to the local hospital.'

'Who is coming through the courtyard? Anchu *Dadu*...'

The two brothers listened hard.

'I have brought some rice and curry for you. Eat it.'

'Where was our father shot, *Dadu*?' Sandhyamani broke down in Anchu *bura*'s arms. 'They say if you are shot at your legs, you will live but if you are shot at your chest or stomach, then...'

'Don't cry. Eat something. Since morning you haven't eaten...'

'Why did they shoot my father, *Dadu*? What did he do? Why are bullets fired every year, *Dadu*? Why?'

She cried profusely.

SIX

The brothers fell asleep after eating the meal brought by Anchu *bura*. He had stayed back and now sat dozing. The lamp was burning still. All kinds of night birds were calling, their cries ghostly.

Nobody was sure where Father was shot. Not even the union Babu was sure. Where was Pocha shot? Pocha succumbed to it. Who fired the bullet? The police, wasn't it? People were saying if there was a lockout, even our ration will stop; but if Father died? They say my father's father was also shot because he demanded a bonus.

The little girl had to grow up fast.

'Father?'

'What?'

Sandhyamani was returning with sweets from the Talapshal market. 'Nothing.'

'If I get a bonus for *Pujo*, I will buy you a new dress.'

'A Lasa.'

'What is a Lasa?'

'*Arey*, haven't you seen them in the TV? Even the Saheb's daughter wears it.'

'Okay. I will buy you a Nasa.'

'It is not a Nasa. Lasa.'

Whenever she got any time, she ran to watch TV in the club. So many wonderful serials, beautiful people with pomp and glamour! Happiness seemed to overflow out of the TV screen. A long breath pierced out of her chest and spread over her little body. A civet cat barked suddenly. The wild smell of its body spread everywhere. Sandhyamani tiptoed out to the courtyard. The bird perched on the blackberry tree flew away. Sandhyamani could feel the fluttering of its wings. The sky was still bereft of stars. How suffocating! Sandhyamani gazed up at the sky.

'Sandhyamani?'

Her eyes fixed at the sky, she murmured, 'Hmm?'

Anchu *bura* had come out too. The two figures stood near each other, unable to see each other's faces in the stuffy darkness.

'Don't cry. Won't you call me...Anchu Anchu...?'

'You call out...'

'It's your thing. How can I do it?'

'Nothing can happen. Call.'

'Anchu *Bura*...Anchu Anchu...Kadi Badamchu...'

But Sandhyamani was way beyond him! How deftly she ran through the darkness! Through the forests of *sirish*, she ran as she seemed to have grown into a woman from a little girl. The fiery red flowers beneath her feet were sobbing out loud. The bonus bullets were raining all around! The *Pujo* drums could be heard. The dark pools of blood stop Anchu *bura* from looking around him. Spread through the universe, Sandhyamani was plastered within a gigantic frame. The darkness was giving way to light. Birds were chirping. Like an intoxicated person, Anchu *bura* kept chasing Sandhyamani but he was quite unable to reach her. Unable to reach...

Translated by Aishwarya Banerjee and Debjani Sengupta

THE BOY

ONE

On the banks of the large lake, Padmabeel, beside the green hillocks, the boy with the emaciated legs used to mow grass. He would crawl into the water and pluck the lotus flower sometimes, drawing it near to him with a bamboo. Sometimes he would eat the stalk of the flower. The boy would also graze the cows by crawling on his sickly legs.

'Why do you work so hard?'

'If I sit idle, who will feed me, *bolo*. Say?'

My eyes would well up with tears! Really, he was a boy who belonged to the poorest of the poor! Who would feed him? He must have been twelve or thirteen years old. The boy would play his flute while grazing the cows. The notes would reverberate among the green hillocks, the waters of Padmabeel and in the leaves of the trees.

'What happened to your legs?'

'Mother said that I was not like this at birth. I had the strength of an *asur* in my limbs. One day, I had fever and look what happened after that! Do you know what my mother says?'

'What does she say?'

'A witch has cast a spell on me.'

'A witch?'

'Yes, a witch. After that I wore so many amulets…trying to exorcise the evil spirit through charms and incantations…'

'No, it is not a witch. Probably your feet…'

'What?'

'Never mind. What work does your father do?' I asked with a long sigh.

'Father has gone to Haflong to work on the roads.'

'And your mother?'

'Mother plucks tea leaves now.'

Suddenly a storm blew up in the clouded sky. I watched amazed as the boy shepherded the cows together, crawling this way and that!

TWO

Today the sky was mostly clear. Autumn had arrived. I saw the boy plucking *dheki* saag near the spring.

'What are you doing?'

'Plucking the fern. I'll go home and cook these.'

'Can I ask you something?'

'What?' The boy looked straight up at me.

'Do you want to go to school?'

'I studied for two classes. After that...'

A wild pigeon came flying and began to peck on the ground. The boy returned to his plucking. I felt a great sadness. In the sky, white patches of clouds floated by. A bunch of butterflies, countless bulbuls, black-hooded orioles and long-tailed birds flitted all around. The boy didn't look at any of them. Why wouldn't he look?

THREE

Some children were playing near the *dhoopghar*, the large shed where tea leaves were dried. The boy watched them play. He didn't smile or talk to them. He wore too large a shirt; also torn. Mother had told him that she would buy him a new one after getting wages. That was a year back.

'It's getting dark. What are you doing?'

The boy didn't answer.

'Where's your mother?'

'She went to the market to buy sweets for my brother and sister.'

'And for you?'

The boy was silent.

'Has she bought clothes for *Pujo*?'

'Yes, for my brother and sister.'

'And for you?'

This time too he remained silent.

'Why do you not speak?'

'Mother said what was the use of new clothes for me? Would I go to see the image of the Goddess?'

Back home, I sat with my mind racing. I couldn't concentrate on any work. Neither could I sleep at night. Two thin legs had touched my nerves and spread a thin crust of melancholy all over my body. I tossed about restlessly, in a torment. Early in the morning, I met the boy beside the lake.

He was sitting silently under the *jarul* tree. A wild pigeon was flapping its wings nearby. I placed my hand on his head. He lifted his face with trust. The pigeon flew away. The boy was smiling through his tears. The early dew of an autumn dawn washed his emaciated legs. Maybe for the first time, his twelve-year-old lungs breathed in the fragrance of the *seuli* flowers. I noticed that he had lifted his head to look up at the sky...

Translated by Kallol Choudhury and Debjani Sengupta

THE WITCH

A body is burning. It is being burnt, you know; not just burning. That too a breathing, live body. The smoke is oozing out in coils towards the sky. The stench of burnt human flesh is unfurling on every facet of the sky, the lake, the hills and the rice fields. It is spreading into human consciousness, flowing rapidly through their blood and veins. The heart-wrenching wail that emanated from the helplessly burning body pierced the ears a few times. Now, everything has calmed down. Deadened. The exuberance of the people has also come to a standstill. Some are still pondering whether Dukhiya Dhai was really a witch. But why the question? Certainly, she was. So many little boys have fallen prey to her bloodthirst. So many people's hearts have been eaten by her. *Have you seen it*? What if I have not? Ramu has seen. Mohan has seen.

She has even adored and loved you. Did you forget, Mohan? During that epidemic, when you were battling for your life, who do you think sat beside you all night? Who do you think brought back Shyamrati's son from the river? Who do you think nurtured you people? Isn't Dukhiya someone's *pishi, mashi* or *didi*? Could you, people of Shyampur, possibly pay back what you owe to Dukhiya? Above all, Dukhiya was your *dhai*, the village midwife. It was her hands that brought you to this earth. Don't you know a *dhai* is no less than a mother? And you burnt her alive! Can every one of you vouch from the heart of your hearts that Dukhiya was a witch? Can you? Swear on yourself. Can you? You cannot.

What if her skin had sagged, her eyes had sunk into their sockets? What if she had learnt a bit of incantations and indulged herself in some spells? Almost everyone had sought her help. The doctor's wife from the city, the local teacher, police…everyone sought the benefits Dukhiya had to offer and today, each one of you stood, watched and enjoyed her death! You know her son lives in the city. Works in a gas factory. He did not come. You know he had acquired five degrees. He used to read a lot of books. He wasn't supposed to leave the village. It was the villagers who exiled him. Why wouldn't they! Wasn't he the one who used to claim that he doesn't believe in caste, doesn't believe in religion? He even went to the extent of eating in a *chamar* household. At that time, the only TV in Shyampur belonged to Mahendra Babu and the *Ramayana* was being telecast.

After his bath, when Mahendra Babu used to sit before the TV with a lighted incense stick, making a show of his spirituality, Dukhiya's son used to comment, 'Bloody hypocrite!' When the local MLA came during elections to rig votes, the boy was aggressive and ready to give him a blow. Thank God, the people had restrained him. Mahendra Babu was not the kind of man who would tolerate such impudence for long. Thus, the villagers had banished the boy.

Dukhiya had called her son, 'Please, come back, the people are calling me a witch. You can do farming here.'

'It won't be possible for me to leave my job, Ma. Better come and stay with me.'

'But how can I ever leave my ancestors' land, Son?'

'Then I'll come, just wait for a few more days.'

The words had made Dukhiya weave a string of hope. From then on, evenings passed into nights, nights gave way to days. One by one, the months crossed the threshold of a year; Dukhiya's wait for her son continued. His father too had left home one day, never to return. Is the boy exactly like his father? Dukhiya's heart would feel an uneasy restlessness.

All day, Dukhiya sat outside with her legs stretched out. The downpour had finally receded, replacing the grey sky with blue. The blackberry tree at the corner of the courtyard was bent with ripe fruits. The guava trees were also laden. A pair of squirrels were hopping around the trees and enjoying a meal of ripe guavas. None of the village children came to eat those fruits. Really, who would dare to visit a witch's house? Earlier they would come in surging numbers during this season and would not go even after several lashings of her tongue. All of it was Dukhiya's misfortune.

Two kids were passing by chatting loudly along the street. Dukhiya wanted to call out to them. However, she could not. It made her heart churn.

That morning too was a bright sunny one when Dukhiya was sitting with her legs splayed out. It was Bhadra from the neighbouring village who had suggested to her, 'We both have grown old, now it's time we learnt some spells.'

'Spells? What would I do with spells?'

'Why? You can make some pendant *tabiz* and sell them.'

'But I do not want to harm people,' Dukhiya had said.

'Why would you harm people? You would help them. By the power of your charm pendants, by the power of your incantations, the sick will be healed, the childless will be blessed with child.'

Some of it did come true. The local teacher's wife was blessed with a boy after she wore the charm offered by Dukhiya. However, Dukhiya now realised that the boy would have come anyway, it had nothing to do with her spells.

Bhadra had further suggested, 'Listen, you need to go through some initiation rituals as well.'

Dukhiya, unable to surmise the strange offer, had asked, 'Initiations? What are they?'

'You have to walk naked with a bowl of oil to the hillock of Shonmari and offer your puja to Maa Tara.'

Hearing this, Dukhiya's heart had pounded.

'Don't you worry, just try to have some courage in your heart.'

A plum-headed parakeet perched on the guava tree. Dukhiya set out the mattresses under the sun. It had been ages since they were aired. Nowadays, nothing really interested Dukhiya. It had been ages since she had applied oil on her hair; they had soon turned into dreadlocks. It seemed all her worries were winding down the pathways of her mind. She stared at the sky…'Just try to have some courage in your heart.' The words made Dukhiya laugh now.

She did bring some courage into her heart. She did go naked with Bhadra to the hillock of Shonmari on a new moon night. Dukhiya had felt the eerie ambience with all her consciousness. She did prescribe people *kavach* and *tabiz* for a while. She was encumbered with a weird sense of optimism those days. But how long could you keep these things secret?

Some said that Dukhiya was seen dancing near the river with her open locks kissing the breath of air. Others claimed that Dukhiya was seen drinking a child's blood. Some had also seen Dukhiya strolling at night around the burning ghat, naked. And all of a sudden, Jyoti's son had died of blood dysentery. Why wouldn't he? They did not provide him with any medicines. But everybody blamed Dukhiya. What about the disease? It was an eye-wash. The witches knew all kinds of charms. Mohan vouched that he himself had witnessed Dukhiya entering Jyoti's house. Now, everyone began to be afraid of Dukhiya. Mothers started shooing their kids away from her. Everyone avoided her except for Shyamrati and Pocha who refused to believe that Dukhiya was a witch. Dukhiya cursed her fate. Why on earth had Bhadra led her on? It was just for a single day that Dukhiya went naked to offer her puja. And she had practiced her charms only for a few times in all these years. She never intended to harm people. Now when she went out, little kids followed her, calling, 'Here goes the witch. Dukhiya has become a witch.' All the jeering silently burnt Dukhiya's heart.

She yearned for her son. It had been ages since she had seen him. 'Oh, my dearest.'

'What?' Dukhiya's son did not move his eyes from his book.

'I often see a dream.'

'What kind of a dream?' the boy had asked with a frown.

'That I am running away to a faraway land on a white horse holding you to my breast.'

'Where?'

'To a snowy white world.'

Her son had smiled.

'Don't you see the dream too?'

'No Ma, I do not have any such dreams.'

A few other children of Shyampur had died without proper medical facilities. Everybody said that it was Dukhiya who was killing them and she must be driven out of the village. Tears rolled down incessantly from Dukhiya's eyes.

'See, the witch is crying.'

'Those are tears of bewitchment which they use to deceive people.'

All her life Dukhiya had thought about others. How could people forget everything within a few days like it had never happened? Dukhiya snivelled in pain. She was starving and although she had rice in her kitchen, she didn't feel like getting up to cook.

Dukhiya owned 8 *bighas* of land, a part of which was cultivated by Pocha Bauri. If untouched by flood or drought, the rice field yielded sufficient amount to sustain her. It was not in Dukhiya's nature to beg for anything. There was a time when Dukhiya used to grow vegetables like *lau, jhinge* and *begun* in her own garden. Then she would happily share her produce with her neighbours. She had never charged a paisa from them. And today she was shunned by all! Dukhiya's father had adored her; she was his favourite. After her parents had lost six children, Dukhiya was born and survived. Her father had named her Dukhiya, the one touched by sorrow. Then he would say, 'I will never let despair touch my Dukhiya.'

The sky was overcast with fluffy clouds that one would generally see with the arrival of autumn, *Sarat*.

'What happened, dear? Didn't you like your saree for *Pujo*?' her mother enquired while sweeping the floor. 'Tell me what kind of a saree would you like? *Siliker*? We will get you whatever you like.'

That promise would make Dukhiya smile. Her father and mother would also join in her mirth. Her father had left a bit of land for Dukhiya. He even found a husband for her, a *ghor jamai*, who would stay with her parents. However, one day, a sudden sense of self-respect made the man change. Dukhiya's son was just two at that time. After that, Dukhiya's parents tried till their last breath to settle her in a second marriage but to no avail as she decided not to remarry. She used to say, 'My life is fine. I grow vegetables in my own farm, the land yields enough rice for me to sustain myself. I work as a midwife and it is by my hands that new lives are brought into this world. I have a lovely child who is already enrolled in school. What else do I need?'

However, Dukhiya's precious son was the one who did not return after venturing out to the city. Hopefully, he didn't become a vagrant like his father! Nonetheless, her husband, the boy's father, had appeared to love Dukhiya. He never misbehaved with her. He used to take her to the fair. Once, even to the *jatra*. He had also taken her to the cinema in town; but his laziness and ego prevented him from getting along well with his father-in-law. So, he had fled. He had an inclination towards music. Dukhiya heard that he worked now with some kirtan group, playing dhol for them.

She stares at the sky. The heat of the sun is overbearing. Her stomach is churning with hunger. Dukhiya lights a fire and starts to cook some rice. Beside the courtyard, mustard leaves have bloomed. Those too are Dukhiya's creation. Dukhiya picks up a few leaves and chops them. Oh! She has run out of salt. Jadav's shop is not far away. Almost everything is available in his shop: rice, pulses, oil, salt, tobacco, matches, biscuit, sugar, tea leaves, toys, bangles, hair ribbons, even wire. Most of his business ran on credit. He is a good man and offers loans. However, he leaves no stone unturned to collect his money. He shows much respect to Dukhiya but how can she go to Jadav's shop? The incessant catcalls, 'The witch, the witch,' would encumber Dukhiya as soon as she stepped out.

The rice is boiling. The fragrance acts as an appetizer to Dukhiya's hungry stomach.

It has been days that she has cooked for her child.

'Ma…Maa.'

Dukhiya, leaving aside her threshing, gets up to see her son standing with a pile of *kajallata* in his hands.

'Take it Ma. Make a curry, please.'

'You dared to get inside the pond…Don't you know they are infested with snakes.'

The boy smiles.

'I was passing by the Shonmari road. My eyes caught sight of the *kajallata* on the pond. I just couldn't resist the temptation, you know.'

'Of course! I will cook for you.'

Unfortunately, Dukhiya never got a chance to cook the *kajallata* for her son. They eventually dried up. And then had arrived the ominous moment of the boy's banishment. 'I would cook for you some other day, my son'; but the boy did not come back from the city.

The rice is burning. The water in it has dried up. Dukhiya hurriedly takes down the rice and puts a wok on the stove. With a little oil, she starts cooking the leaves.

'What are you cooking, *Pishi*?' Shyamrati comes panting.

'Just some mustard leaves, dear. I am starving.'

'*Pishi*, please run away from the village as soon as possible.'

'Why? Why would I run away from my ancestral land?'

'There was a meeting where it was decided that they would burn you to death. As soon as I heard the news, I came to warn you.'

Dukhiya laughs.

'Don't laugh! Please run away, *Pishi*.'

Pocha too comes running. 'Run away, *Didi*.'

Dukhiya laughs again.

'Don't laugh, *Didi*. Come with me. You don't know these people. They change colours so quickly. They are capable of anything. Let's go.'

'I am famished. Let me eat some rice first.'

'Go ahead. Eat.'

Dukhiya takes the rice on a bronze plate.

The crowd has swelled. 'Don't let the witch get away.'

'At least let her have a morsel of rice,' Shyamrati implores.

The burning heat of the sun is overhead. The call of a spotted dove can be heard from some far corner of the forest. Piercing the hollow tin chest of the mob was a cry: 'Where are you taking me? When will my son return?' They doused Dukhiya's body with kerosene and set her ablaze. Shyamrati screams in terror. Pocha runs towards the police chowki. The mob rejoices.

Dear mob, aren't you the same people who organise revolutions at places? Aren't you the people who put despotic rulers behind the bars? And at places, you rejoice after burning women like Dukhiya? Dukhiya's body continues to burn. The stench of burnt human flesh is unfurling on every aspect of the sky, the lake, the hills and the rice fields. It is spreading deep into human consciousness, flowing through their blood and veins. As she burnt, Dukhiya remembers her father's face, her mother's visage, and in the end, she sees the vision, riding a white horse with her little son, in search of a white world.

Dukhiya Dhai's erudite son returns from the city one day. He smells the stench of burnt flesh in the soil and in the air. When he tries to stretch his spine, he finds a vast firmament above him. Under it, he falls to his knees. He too sees his mother's dream today: riding a white horse with her, aloft the cotton clouds, they are voyaging in search of a white world. Far, far away.

Translated by Aishwarya Banerjee and Debjani Sengupta

ENCEINTE WOODLANDS

Listening to the cuckoo's repetitive calls, Sonaram's wife cooks rice, feeding the fire with the dry leaves of the jackfruit tree. Last evening, she had spent a long time collecting them. After the rice is done, the remaining leaves may just be enough to cook the tender shoots of the fern. Early in the morning she had picked those tender green leaves. Close to the woodlands, their house is built with bamboos and thatched grass. It is risky to use dry leaves to build a fire, but she cooks with them. While cooking, her whole being trembles, as her father-in-law sits close by, talking.

'O *Bou*, have you heard it?'

'What?'

'There was something in the newspaper.'

'What? What was written there?' Picking some dry leaves in her folded palms, she turns her head.

'Four people were released who had been with Barada Babu. But tell me, my child, what happened to my Sonaram?'

The old man's throat starts to make a rumbling noise with his effort to speak. He probably wants to talk some more but cannot.

From her folded palms, she drops the dry leaves as the dying fire comes back to life and the rice in the pot starts to bubble. *Yes, what really happened to Sonaram?* Since the day he had gone to the jungle with Barada Babu, he never returned. After that day, she has lost count of time; night has turned into day and day into night. The months and the years rolled by but Sonaram never came back. Actually, they had come to know after two days that terrorists had abducted them. It was also rumoured that Barada Babu's children had paid a ransom. How come they were not released? Now four people have been freed, but why not Sonaram?

Holding Sonaram's hand, she had left lane number eight of Dhalai garden—leaving behind Kukicherra and Jugicherra—to arrive at this place: Ram Shantipur, next to this reserved forest. After seeing this thick forest, she had almost lost her mind. She used to roam around there alone, so often! Such gigantic trees! And coiling around them, countless varieties of wild creepers trailed up! She would feel intoxicated smelling the wild fragrance of the trees and the plants! Even during the day, foxes would peep around. She had seen a cheetah, twice. She had also seen the lustful hungry eyes of the forest guard. But she was unable to give up her obsessive jungle adventures. The woodlands had taken her mind and spirit in its grip.

The cuckoo is still calling. Her old father-in-law calls her again. 'O *Bou*...*Bou*.'

'What is it now?'

'Can you give me a little juice of the tulsi leaves?'

'I will. But I'll make some tea first and you can have some.'

The old man feels happy when he hears about the tea. His sunken eyes shine. It was a long time ago that he used to feed the machine with the raw green leaves while filling his lungs with the aroma of the fresh tea. And one day, while swallowing the leaves, the machine swallowed a part of his right hand too. The Saheb paid for his medical care. He also got the compensation money, but that did not come for a few years. Was Sonaram born then? No, he was not born yet. With the compensation money, he had bought the land and hut, next to the reserved forest, from Pakhi Miah. Oh, that was a long time ago! There was no terrorist problem at that time. Except the bossy forest guards, there had been no problem.

The cuckoo calls out again. His daughter-in-law brings the tea in a glass and with loud thud, puts it near him.

'Now, drink.'

'Isn't there any milk?'

'No. Can't find the goat, so couldn't milk it in the morning. Don't know where it has wandered away.'

Last year, two kids were mauled by wolves. The jackals and the wolves just lie in wait for the cattle to come out of the barn.

The chickens too fill the bellies of the wild cats and the foxes. Sometime ago, they had dragged a few straight out of the barn. That time, Sonaram had brought a puppy from Jhalancherra. See how he guards the house! The foxes will run away with their tails between their legs! They gave him a name: Kala. As long as Kala was there, they didn't lose even one chick or one kid. But Kala had been missing since Sonaram was abducted. Who knows where Kala is now? The bird is calling again. A fox peeps out of a bush and ducks back again.

She takes off the pot of rice from the stove and stokes the fire with some leaves. Now the green fern leaves must be fried. She puts the iron skillet on the fire. Sonaram loved to eat these leafy vegetables. So she used to pick those tender shoots often.

The old man garbled out: 'Fry those leaves, dear. I'd like to eat them with a roti. My mother used to cook them with black gram.'

'Hey. Listen.'

'What?'

'You roam around the forest all the time. Aren't you afraid at all?'

She used to laugh. Giggling, she used to reply, 'These trees, these creepers…they smell so good. I feel like hugging them.'

'You are like the jungle too,' Sonaram used to say while drawing her into a tight embrace.

'Believe me, I am telling the truth,' she used to reply, pulling him closer.

'And if someday the forest guard...?' Sonaram used to whisper to her...

'O *Bou*! *Bou*!'

'I am coming now.'

The iron skillet is red hot. She pours the oil into it, drop by drop.

'O! You dark skinned maiden, I hear your name so often
In the bungalow of the white planter you bloom like a flower,
The white skinned man is a loser
Shame! Shame on you girl!'

As a little girl, she used to sing this song while eating the fried seeds of a *cham* fruit while the acacia flowers underneath her feet had cried their benediction.

'Oye, why don't you give me a few more seeds?'

'Why don't you go and collect some? Around the number ten siding, there are plenty under the trees…'

'Why do you talk so much? Give me a few.'

'Okay. Take some.' The girl had giggled and had offered some nuts to Fulmoni.

The acacia flowers had laughingly whispered, 'Wow! Look at that green pigeon, sitting on that branch, how it flapped its wings!'

'O *Bou*!'

'What happened?' As she picks up the ladle, she is surprised when she turns her eyes towards the jungle. *Good heavens, Fazal Ali and Ripan Das are coming this way*! Taking the metal ladle in her left hand, she covers her head quickly. Her old father-in-law sits up after another round of heavy coughing.

'Listen, we talked with the Reang terrorists.'

'What did you talk about?'

'They said they would release Sonaram if you give them 25,000 rupees.'

'Where would we get such a huge sum?'

'Why! You have your land.'

'You mean, sell our land?'

'No. No. Take a mortgage. You can get your land back.'

'But they did not release Barada Babu even after getting the money.'

'He is a different case. There are reasons.'

'Reasons? What reasons?'

'Forget it. It is politics. You will not understand, *Bou*.'

She says, 'I'll go to the local assembly member.'

'Haven't you gone to him twice? What happened?'

'I'll go again.'

The woman fixes her gaze on the far-lying woodlands and tears flood her eyes. After Sonaram was abducted, the two ploughing bulls got foot and mouth disease and died. Her old father-in-law had lamented, 'I was better off as a labourer. I don't know why I purchased this land to come here.'

In the beginning, the police, CRP, journalists, so many came and went. Even the member of the legislative assembly came once, with many words of hope. And now? Everybody remains quiet!

The fire in the oven has died a while ago. The leaves in the skillet have withered. *What a fate,* thinks the woman. The jungle is full of firewood, yet she is forced to cook rice using leaves. The cuckoo is cooing again. With the ladle in her hand, the woman stays still. Durga *Pujo* is coming soon. Narayan Paul is constructing the idol with hay. Every year, he is the one to do so. Before him, his father Gostha Paul used to make the idol. And before him, his grandfather. This woman, a little girl then, used to spend the whole day in the *thakur dalan*.

She used to observe everything: the structure made with hay and bamboo, then the plastering of the clay over it and finally the painting of the eyes. In her unbridled excitement, she used to forget her games, her sleep, her meals. It was on the seventh or the eighth day of that special month, as Subal was playing the drums, that her father, Sudhanya, had taken away her beloved little goat for sacrifice to the Goddess. He had a vow to fulfil. She had run away crying and hid herself in the lonely brick yard.

'O *Bou*? *Bou*?'

'Yes, *Baba*. What is it?'

'Tell me, what happened to my Sonaram?'

Exhaling a long breath, leaving the ladle behind, the woman comes out to sit on the ground, spreading her legs, gazing up at the sky. What answer can she give to the old man? So many varieties of clouds float in the sky. And what a wide range of colours they have! She remembers the Goddess

Manasa when she sees the clouds. Goddess Manasa and the clouds, then clouds and Manasa—somehow, everything gets intertwined. Her father used to say, 'I have pledged the bananas in her name; she is very powerful. Don't eat them.' And her mother used to say, 'I am making *muri* for her, don't touch them.' Songs used to fill the evenings of the rainy month of *Shravana*, making it all feel so magical. Step by step, she retreats into the past. Behula's song rings in her ears—

> With a raft of banana stems, I will go to Ujani Nagar,
> Floating on the waters, carrying my dead beloved…

'O *Bou*? *Bou*?'

'I am here, *Baba*…'

There is an investigation going on, related to the abduction of Barada Babu; but nobody remembers Sonaram. Selling the pregnant goat at last, the woman went to the nearby town to visit the political leaders to seek their help. But nobody took notice of her. What did Ripan Das and others do with the money after selling the land? Nobody knows.

Last night a lonely water bird hopped throughout. The woman could not sleep at all, thinking of Sonaram. The dawn broke. She stepped out towards the jungle. Such big trees! So many creepers and vines—in the past few days of rain, they have grown faster. Soaking in the rain-fed air, the woman moved further in. Wild, earthy aroma slowly started to engulf her body…a tremor of joy spread through her pores. At one point, the deep enceinte woodlands started to embrace her, the way Sonaram used to. Getting wet in the rain, the woman slowly lost herself in the wild redolence of the jungle. Who knew so much love was dispersed in this woodland? The dripping noise of the falling rain on the leaves filled the air. Covered with water droplets, mud, vines and creepers, she laid herself down there, holding the comforting tinge of the forest in her womb.

Maybe the woman will give birth to another forest…The trees and the bushes, the birds and the creatures are laughing out loud…

By then will Sonaram have come back?

Translated by Mohan L. Zaigirdar

SISIRKONA WILL PLAY ON

After many years, Sisirkona took out her dust covered sitar and sat with it. Lovingly, she dusted the instrument and feathered her fingers over the strings after wearing the rusty *mizrab* on the index finger of her right hand. After years, Sisirkona was immersed in creating rhythm on her sitar and as she plucked the strings, they danced in happiness and pure glee.

The courtyard was filled with marigold plants: yellow, orange, yellow mixed with dark brown...oh, the colours were resplendent. To protect them from the cattle, her husband, Hemkrishna, had made fences with bamboo stakes all around. An unknown bird kept calling, again and again. Dewdrops kept falling outside: *tup*, *tup*, *tup*, *tup*... falling from the coconut leaves, the custard apple leaves, the fig leaves, from the tin roof and from the memories and the pain of her heart—Sisirkona was going to make melody out of it all.

Sisirkona was playing music: a small girl, with plaits tied firmly on two sides of her head, wearing a red georgette frock with white lace that had been refashioned from one of her mother's saris. A sliver of morning ray came to light up her dress.

'Listen, tune the main string in the front to the middle note and the other strings to...'

'Kona...Kona...Sisirkona,' Her mother, Probhaboti, had come to call but left when she saw her daughter engrossed in her instrument. A smell of turmeric wafted from her mother's sari...

'Listen carefully to all the notes that I am playing...Sa, Re, Ga, Ma...This is a difficult raga...'

'Kona...Kona, I have served lunch,' Probhaboti came to stand near her daughter.

'I have told you not to disturb us when the lessons are on,' Her father had been angry as he had taken off the *mizrab* from his index finger.

'Alright, I won't,' said Probhaboti, as she left the room.

Sisirkona had been an attentive pupil when she had learnt all the ragas and the rhythms from her father. She had learnt them along with another disciple, Sashidhar. She remembered it had been winter and the dewdrops kept falling on the stalks of rice plants outside their home. Scores of bees were flying about in search of nectar. And then the earth had heaved, and kept on shaking for four or five days. What a turmoil it had been; that earthquake of the 50's! That tremor could still be felt now and then! An unknown bird kept on calling. Why was she feeling cold? Sisirkona wrapped the shawl around her. That winter, *Ostad* Moti Mian had visited their home. She never knew how the night had vanished in the melody that he had created.

'You will be great one day, my daughter.'

'How great, *Ostad* ji?'

'Great, really great,' Moti Mian had assured her as Sisirkona had looked at him with widened eyes. But all of *Ostad* ji's wishes had come to naught. The sitar had soon vanished from her hands.

One early morning Sisirkona was playing Raga Bhairavi, when her mother had fallen ill. There had been no time to call a doctor. For many days, she would catch a waft of the turmeric smell that had been so much a part of her mother. She had immersed herself in her practice: day in and day out, she had played her sitar while Sashidhar had played the tabla in unison. Sisirkona had felt no tiredness: the *dhamar* and the *keherwa* would dance through her artist fingers; the *gat*, or the precomposed section, would end and the *aalaap* would begin as her fingers flew incandescent over the sitar strings. She had performed in many music programmes and people had lauded her playing. She had been invited to play at Shillong Radio and had been ready to go when someone sent an anonymous letter alleging all kinds of scandalous things. Sisirkona had been terribly upset as her father had arranged her match with Hemkrishna, the school teacher. Oh, a string had come undone on her sitar! She set to tie it again…

In one fell stroke, her beloved sitar had been displaced from her lap. Sisirkona had pleaded with her father but her tears were in vain. Then, one by one, her lap had been filled with five children, and Sisirkona had no time to play her sitar. Where was Sashidhar now? Maybe he was old just like Sisirkona? She breathed out loud. The mist was slowly lifting. The morning sun fell gently on the orange flowers. After many years, Sisirkona suddenly smelt the soft turmeric smell of her mother's sari. The sweet morning rays had reached the veranda, flooding the sitar on her lap. Far away, the Lusai hills were also shinning in the magical light. Sisirkona had finished tuning her instrument; she was now ready to play. Breathing deep, she filled her lungs with the smell of memories and dreams and looked at the beautiful marigolds in the sun. A smile slowly lit up her face as she resolved that Sisirkona would play…she would play on.

Translated by Debjani Sengupta

OOZING

Sonoka's five-feet body lay on a torn blanket. She was dead. Her swollen left hand that looked like a thigh was teeming with flies. Both the eyes were shut. Some clothes were hanging from a string inside the windowless room. A cat was sniffing at some stale rice on a plate. A few vessels were scattered here and there. Some green leafy vegetable lay in a corner. Sonoka's black dog was lying still near the door. This had first attracted the attention of Lakshmi. She was passing by to fetch water from the spring. Noticing the door open, she had peeped into the room and had called Sonoka by name, 'Are you going to stay inside today, Sonokabhoji?'

Getting no response, Lakshmi went inside the room and was shocked when she touched Sonoka's body. Who knew when she had died! With still eyes, Lakshmi gazed at the dead woman. Then taking a cloth from the rope, she covered the body. A sudden cold fear made Lakshmi turn away from the room. She came and sat on the grass under the *jarul* tree that was covered with violet flowers. Tears rolled down her eyes but she didn't wipe them off. Her parched lips tasted salty.

Lakshmi had known that it might happen one day. A bird flew away from the *jarul* with a flap of its wings. Nearby, on the marshy lowland, there were clusters of creepers and edible aquatic plants. One or two egrets were flying about. A waterbird sat idle. Earlier, there was a big lake at that place, with overflowing water. Abundant water lilies drew many people. It was rumoured that fairies came in droves, mad with the scent of flowers. Although Lakshmi hadn't seen any fairies in her childhood, when she came to collect the stalks of the water lily, she would spit at her own breast as her mother had told her, to ward off the evil ones. Lakshmi wanted to laugh when she remembered it now. Later, people had built dykes and the water had dried up. A few patches of land grew some crops and people quarrelled over the share of the dry portion of the land. Lakshmi had seen all that. A few dewdrops fell on her forehead from the tree. Lakshmi wiped them with the end of her sari and looked at the road. It was empty except some urchins catching crabs, rummaging through the burrows. Lakshmi signalled to them. The boys came up to her.

'What is it?'

'Do you know Sonokabhoji has died?'

'She would,' one of the boys said callously.

'What do you mean?'

'Why won't she die? Yesterday, *Pisha* has beaten her so much on the very hand with the wound.'

'He beat her the day before her death?'

'Sonoka *Pishi* didn't chop the wood and *Pisha* was drunk.'

'Hurry up and call the others.'

'Is there anyone around now?' The boys were amazed. 'Everyone has gone to work. Don't you see how late it is?'

'I know. Go all the same. I'll be here, *hami ei khine thakbo…*'

The boys looked at each other, speaking a secret language through their eyes, and disappeared. Lakshmi sat down against the *jarul* tree. She was afraid to go into Sonoka's room. Lakshmi was around twenty and Sonoka must have been forty. There was a great deal of difference between twenty and forty and it was a mystery to her how they had been friends!

Nobody knew what had happened to Sonoka's arm. Pus trickled constantly, emitting an odour. Nobody came close to Sonoka. People would put a cloth up to their nostrils whenever she came near. Sonoka too kept away from people. Yet she used to chop wood with the lame hand the whole day. She would buy rice after selling the wood. And she got beaten up by her husband. That fellow was inhuman. Sonoka had gone to the hospital and the doctor had examined her hand with care and prescribed a medicine. She had paid ten rupees to the doctor. She had saved it by hiding it inside a bamboo pole. But where could she get the money to buy medicines? Some had advised her, 'Go to the Medical College for free treatment.' But how could she go to the hospital by boarding a bus? She couldn't. She had got off the bus after she heard the comments of fellow passengers and suffered their irritated glances. She had returned home with a pile of fresh insults and tearful eyes. From then on, she refused to go anywhere. All Sonoka did was go to the jungle and back again to her hut! But Lakshmi, ignoring the foul smell, often came to see her. Sonoka would say, 'Everyone keeps away, including my sister; why do you come? *Tui kene ashis*?'

'I don't feel good if I don't see you.'

'Don't you mind the foul smell?'

'Not at all.'

'Will you tell me a way to die?'

'Do you want to?' Lakshmi had asked after a sigh.

'What's the use of this painful life?'

'I know. I can understand.'

'My mind's pain is much more than that of the body,' Sonoka had said, gasping. 'Yet I have to live with this pain, in this filthy society. There's no one to weep after my death. Will you cry?'

'I'll cry, of course I will.' Lakshmi had promised with her eyes full of glistening tears.

Sonoka's father had been a tenant cultivator and partly a day labourer. Yet in Sonoka's paternal home, she had been cherished and loved. She bought bangles for her wrists when she went to the fair with her father. Sonoka kept fast for the festival of Tusu. What fun her father would have on those days! He would rejoice all night long with friends, drinking *hadiya* the night before Tusu. Sonoka would play Tusu's mother. On the day of the *jagran*, the neighbourhood girls would fast all day and eat a mixture of milk and rice at night; then, they would sing Tusu songs all through the night. The next day, on the day of the *pitha*-eating ceremonies, Sonoka used to immerse the Tusu figurine in the river, after carrying it on her head from one house to another, all the while singing Tusu songs.

Lakshmi's tears dried up. The bird came to sit again on the branch of the *jarul* tree. Where did the *dahuk* go? Gangamani, while passing along the road below, shouted, 'Lakshmi, what are you doing here?'

'Sonokabhoji has passed away.'

'She has died? It is better because she was suffering so much. Where's her husband?'

'Where are you off to?'

'I'm going to the panchayat.'

'Why are you going again? Didn't you win the case against your employer?'

'I've won, but the master has appealed to the judge's court.'

'Why isn't he satisfied?'

'How can that be? When will their desires ever end? But it is my own land; I'm ready to fight for it.'

In the distance, one of the boys, catching crabs, cried out. Both the women looked up, startled.

Gangamani wiped the perspiration from her cheek with a portion of her saree. 'Did you inform others?'

'I have,' Lakshmi said.

'I can't stay. Tomorrow is my hearing. I'll board a vehicle from the panchayat office. I'll not be able to appear at the right time if I don't go a day early to town.'

'Go if you have to.'

Gangamani left. Lakshmi thought she should put an end to all the devils one day. She had taught Ashim Babu's son a good lesson the day before yesterday. He used to follow her around for days. She had collected dry wood from the jungle that day. She had stood still when she heard a rustling sound from the dense bush near the marshes. Ramu had come out from behind the bush. Lakshmi, keeping down the pile of wood, had stood up straight. Then she had fixed her eyes on him.

'Tell me why do you keep following me?'

'Oh, I mean…I like you very much.'

'It matters little if you like me. Will you marry me? Will you put a vermilion mark on my forehead in the presence of others?'

'No, no, how can that be?'

'How can that be!' Lakshmi had thrown a threatening look at Ramu.

'Listen, I'll give you money and a sari.'

'Are you tempting me?' Her stare became more intense. 'Listen, we may be labourers, but we have more self-respect than you people. Understand?' Taking out a gleaming machete from the pile of wood, she had thrown it at Ramu. She had then walked off with the bundle of firewood on her head. Today morning, Lakshmi had seen Ramu enter Nabin's shop dragging his injured leg. How Lakshmi hated the filth of society! The prime enemy of man was a man who turned everything dirty. Why did people spread scandalous rumours about others? But they did. Why did they do something to ruin another? But they did. Lakshmi didn't understand how people had any fun doing all that. She heard some country was at war. Someone had made a kind of bomb that could only kill people without disturbing anything all around. To fulfil their foul desires, their greed, lust, revenge and hunger, humans throttled other humans. What a strange world!

Lakshmi felt a great pain in her breast. Why didn't man look at the flowers? Why didn't they listen to the chirping of birds and look at the moving clusters of clouds? Lakshmi was reminded, all of a sudden, of a face: a fair-complexioned, unblemished face. It seemed she would remember that face throughout her life. Who knew where that stranger had come from. Lakshmi had liked that person very much. As much as she liked flowers, moonlight, hillocks. The stranger had asked, 'What do you love?'

'I love flowers, hills, river and springs.'

'And?'

'And good people.'

'Do you know humans undergo great suffering?'

'Suffering?'

'Yes, great suffering.'

'One day the suffering will cease.'

'Will it cease? How?'

There was a great deal of happiness in Lakshmi's innocent eyes. That stranger, fixing his look on her face, had said, 'A day will come when everyone's hands would be clenched in fists.'

Lakshmi had found the idea difficult to understand. The stranger had said goodbye to her.

'Please come again.'

'Why do you say so?'

'I don't know.'

The stranger had sighed and gone away. Whenever the pain in Lakshmi's heart increased, that immaculate face appeared before her. Her pain turned instantly to joy.

Midday had come to an end. The sunlight looked like an elderly pale woman. In the marshy land below, sadness had gathered, just like in Lakshmi's heart. Fluttering their wings, the cranes went flying. A kingfisher sat idle, like the emptiness all around.

Some people gathered and built a *machan* with bamboos. Sonoka's man was there too. Lakshmi sat and watched all that activity. Her heartache increased with the sound of cutting of bamboos. Lakshmi knew that a little later Sonokabhoji would be laid on the *machan* and carried to the cemetery ground. They would dig a burial pit and put her into it. Tall weeds would grow over the mound and days later, if Lakshmi looked that way, her heart would ache. Lakshmi suddenly thought: Sonokabhoji would never get off the bus any more. She wouldn't ever ask, 'Will you weep if I die?'

Everybody must die one day. Why couldn't we die peacefully? Who knew when people would hold up their clenched fists? Tears from Lakshmi's eyes trickled down her dark cheeks. Her parched lips tasted salty again.

Translated by Kallol Choudhury

TROUBLED TALES

Moving her fingers slowly through her dry lice-infested hair that resembled jute strands, Kistomoni used two fingers of her right hand to pluck the nits. As she placed one on her left thumb nail to crush it, a series of loud bangs shattered the silence. It seemed to her that a group of devils had emerged from the surrounding darkness! Kistomoni trembled: what was that sound that made her very ribs shake in fear? She had sent her grandson to buy provisions at the grocer's shop; there were so many things that she needed at home. The sounds came from the direction of the shops. Did something happen to the boy? What were the sounds like: bullets and guns firing? Who knew?

'Nirmata? Oh Nirmata!'

Where had she disappeared? A little while ago she was there, cooking greens over the oven and the old woman could smell the frying garlic and red chillies. They lived in a cramped room with a small courtyard, measuring five or six arm-lengths.

It sported a few plants: a gardenia; a few shrubs of chillies, both black and green; a few aubergine plants that produced all the year round. There was a tall creeper of *madhobilata* too; but last year, during the drought in *Baisakh*, it had died, who knew how! Her old man, Haren, the cultivator, was very fond of plants and trees. When they had lived in Motinagar, their old spacious home was surrounded with so many kinds: fruit trees like mango, jamun, jackfruit, fig, *kamranga*...so many of them! The nights were filled with the fragrance of the custard apple flowers! The moringa tree was frequented by a bunch of green parakeets! The *saptaparni* tree, laden with flowers, would make Haren feel intoxicated! He would often call out her name and ask her to come out to smell the air:

'O Kistomoni! *Bairaha*! Come out, Kistomoni.'

'*Kene*? Why? I am cooking!'

Haren would really become restless under that pervading fragrance and he would run about like a mad man! Sometimes he would lie on the rope *khatiya* kept on the courtyard. There would be the *Karam* festival at Radhamoni's room at that time...

You didn't become an Assamese
You didn't become a Bengali
You came to the tea gardens
To become a *Baganiya*...

Their home was filled with greenery but in the end the damming of the river had eaten away their homestead...

Was that a sound of gunfire? Ufff...her heart split in many fragments. That year there was trouble at the tea garden about the *Pujo* bonus. Unlike other times, the police had arrived and had started shooting at the workers. Her father, Jonardon Sardar, had fallen, drenched in blood. Harimoti's *morod* Bibhishon, Sushila's son, Binod, had died too. Her young brother, who had run out to see what was happening, took a bullet too. He hadn't lived many days after being hit!

'O Nirmata...Who's there?'

'It is Kaushalya, *Kaki*. I am Kaushalya.'

'Where is Nirmata? She was here, cooking some greens...'

'Are you dreaming, Aunty? Nirmata is at her in-laws.'

'Nowadays, I forget everything. Did you hear the sound of gunfire?'

'Gunfire? Oh no. They are celebrating the marriage of Ramcharan's son...'

'A wedding? *Shaadi*?'

'Yes, a wedding.'

Her wedding had taken place when she was twelve years old. She had not even reached puberty. She had spent her time playing hide and seek in the *dolu* bamboo jungles when one day she had to wear a fake red silk saree to marry Haren. Over the next four days, the mic had blared a popular Hindi song

'*Pyar kiya toh darna kiya*'—'why should you be afraid to love!' Her father celebrated her wedding with pomp; he had sold off his little bit of land to arrange for the ceremony. He had gifted her a pair of silver anklets and a gold nose-pin.

'Hey Kaushalya...'

'What is it?'

'My grandson has gone out to shop. It is so dark outside, one cannot see one's hand in the pitch blackness...*kemon ashbek bolto*...how will he come back?'

Kaushalya's eyes filled with tears and a few drops escaped down her dark cheeks...one drop, followed by another and then another...

'I had told Nirmata so many times not to leave him behind...Why didn't she listen? "Let him stay," she said. "He can enrol in the school here"... So he went to school. He enjoys studying. He has gone from the *pathsala* to the high school and all his teachers love him...Biman sir used to...O Nirmata... No, no...Kaushalya, have you left?'

'I am here, Aunty.' Kaushalya wiped her eyes as she replied.

'Where is the boy? Why isn't he back?'

'He will come...*ashbek goh*...'

'Isn't it the time for *jitiya*?'

'Yes.'

That year, the boy was born at dawn, during the *jitiya* festival. Her daughter had almost died giving birth. Kistomoni could hear the neighbourhood mothers, after their fasts, singing their way to the river to float the earthen pots into the water...

Rukmini and Radha, two sisters, are off to bathe in the river
How can one describe the beauty of Radha walking?

'Will you eat something, *Kaki*?'

Kistomoni did not answer.

Kaushalya asked again, '*Khabis goh kichu?* There is some rice and smoked *gorui* fish.'

'Yes.'

'Then have something.'

'No, let the boy come back.'

Kaushalya's eyes teared up again. Just a month and a half back, Kistomoni had sent the boy to buy some provisions. It was dusk, just like that day, dark already. She had often done that. Who knew why? Earlier Kistomoni would go herself but lately her eyes had become dim and everything seemed dark to her. Maybe if she had got an operation done she would have been cured. Old Haren had got his done at some government health centre...he had walked around with his bandaged eyes and then they had given him a pair of free spectacles. But... Under the big banyan tree there were a few shops: a tea shop, a grocer's and one for animal feed...

'Oh Kaushalya, did you hear?'

'What?'

'Did you not hear? Gunshots...'

Kaushalya breathed a long sigh. A barn owl called out from Kistomoni's moringa tree.

'Do you know, whenever the owl cried out, the boy would clutch me, tight.'

Kaushalya knew people sold these birds for a lot of money. Sumanta who ran the paan shop had told her so.

'Kaushalya, do you know my grandson loves smoked *gorui* fish. I have cooked some today. Do you want to taste a bit?'

'No Aunty. Not today.'

'You know, the other day, the boy had got some *kauya* fruits and kept saying, "*kha Didi, kha*...have some, Grandma"... I don't know what the boy gets up to!'

Kaushalya glanced outside. It was so dark, yet through that dense darkness, the fragrance from a flowering tree came to her in waves. That day, did the boy remember all that Kistomoni had asked him to buy? A kilo of wheat, a kilo of salt, red chilli powder for two rupees? Who knew? But the thirteen-year-old body was shattered with the bullets that had come from the guns of the extremists...The men had hailed a storm of bullets over the cluster of shops and had vanished. Tomorrow the minister would arrive to give compensation to the families who had lost a dear one. But how was Kaushalya to say that to Kistomoni? Kistomoni was…

Oh no, the old woman had fallen fast asleep on the mud floor and under her closed eyelids two thin streams of tears flowed down. Did she…?

Salty tears crept down Kaushalya's cheeks too. She took a sheet hanging on a rope nearby and covered Kistomoni's sleeping body. She crept out, putting the door on the latch when she heard the gunshots again… *Whose turn was it?* Then she remembered that the evening before, the extremists had kidnapped Kala Mian from Dinanathpur; and the manager of the Patichora tea estate…what was his name? He had been missing too, for so long. Had they killed him off? And the daughter of the manager at the Kalain tea estate…

The barn owl screeched again. The sounds of gunfire pierced the darkness once more. Kaushalya fell to the ground as her head churned. She was covered in mud and dust. She got up and fell again; again and again. Some people were running towards her. She got up and started to flee. It was so dark, not a sliver of light shone anywhere. All those massive feet were now squashing Kaushalya's bones, ribs, her mind and consciousness, the fragrant clean air, Kistomoni's homestead…all were crushed under their feet.

Translated by Debjani Sengupta

PHOOLBASIYA BURI GOES BACK

For some days now, the rain had been falling incessantly… drip, drip, drip. It had no intention to stop. The small canals, ponds, lakes and drains were filled to the brim. The frogs had gone quiet and so had the birds. Not a sound anywhere! Not even the thunder rolled and one only heard the sound of the falling rain. It had become chilly even though a few days ago Phoolbasiya was suffering in the heat. Everyone called her Phoolbasiya *buri*—Phoolbasiya, the old woman. Some others called her *nani* or *dadi*, grandmother! Earlier some others used to call her aunt: she was young then with a head full of black tresses, like the women of the rich houses. When the manager's son had his *mukhjhuta* ceremony there was a big lunch and in the evening, they had *laishabi* songs; they had been wearing such nice dresses, and danced and sang:

The rich women and girls
Have long braids on their backs

Look in the mirror
Tie up their hair…

What wonderful songs they sang! Phoolbasiya too had waist-long hair that came down her back. Those days, she would roam among the tea plants in the Makrichora tea garden while her mother plucked the leaves. Some days, she would carry her mother's rotis if Ma had gone to work hungry. Phoolbasiya would then wander among the tress, picking up the seeds of *cham kathal*. She would bring them home and roast them in a pan. How wonderful they tasted! Here too she had eaten them: Fuchuwa's son would gather them and bring her some! These trees used to cover the small hillocks next to the Bangla *beel* that also had a small forest…This jackfruit was delicious when ripe. Small fleshy seeds, sweet and sour in taste.

When she was young, she could not reach the fruits so high up in the branches. So she would wander beneath the trees in the Makrichora tea garden, hoping that a fruit or two would be lying underneath. Sometimes her two younger brothers were there too! Her two brothers whom she would never see again! Neither would she get any news about them. Were they grown up now? Married with children? Did they remember her? The two boys, Hariya and Biswamitra, were her constant companions as she wandered in the forest and in the jungles, looking for berries and other edible fruits that coloured their tongues dark. They used to go to gather jamun from Sita *mashi*'s hut...they would be strewn all over the courtyard. Sita *mashi* never liked them taking the fruits! One day, Phoolbasiya had planted a jamun tree; it grew up with wonderful branches spread all over! The tree had become Phoolbasiya's friend; it used to wave its branches as soon as she went to stand near it. She would embrace the branches, and rub her cheeks against the leaves. A yellow bird would often sit on its branches; so many other kinds of birds too. But before the tree bore any fruit, Phoolbasiya had to leave.

Did she ever think that the road leading to Makrichora would be shut to her forever? That she would never be able to return there? The jamun tree must have been laden with fruit and all the children must have come to gather them. Alas, Phoolbasiya did not get to see that! It gave her so much pain to think about it. All her life, Phoolbasiya had to carry that pain deep within her. What else could she do?

She would shed copious tears earlier, when she was a young woman. Nowadays, she did not shed any tears anymore; she could not! However, sometimes a drop or two squeezed out and rolled down her wrinkled cheeks. She did not wipe them away. Somewhere they were playing drums and singing songs dedicated to the Goddess Manasa. It must be in the hut of Hari Byakti. She could hear the song clearly:

With red and blue flowers
Garlands made of blood red buds
I will worship you
At your lotus feet…

They worshipped the Goddess at Makrichora too. Some homes had four idols, others had ten…Manasa, Chand Saudagar, Behula, Lakkhindar and so many other. A young Phoolbasiya would sing and fetch water for the rituals. Sudhanya Uncle would hold a thin bamboo stick and worship the idols. He would wear a yellow-coloured dhoti and sit there under the Goddess's influence to become a *bhagat*. People would fall at his feet, praying for health and prosperity. That one day, a *bhagat* would be revered by all! The rituals and worship would take place through the night. The next day, the old idol would be taken out in a procession to be immersed and the new one kept aside. On a crossing, two *bhagat*s would play at being a God amidst a song:

Oh Mother, I am indebted to you
You have fed me with milk
I have not repaid you
Oh Mother, don't leave with tears in your eyes…

The rain had stopped. How late was the night? The unlit kerosene lamp was nearby and she had kept the matchbox near as well. If needed, she would grope for the matchbox and light the lamp. That fellow Sitesh who had become a panchayat president had assured her that they would get her electricity and a home under a government scheme. But that never came true. Those who already had houses made another under the *Indira Awaas* scheme. She didn't have the strength to run around nor to implore them. Didn't they have eyes to see how Phoolbasiya lived? Her roof leaked here and there, and she got drenched often. Her mother-in-law used to say that during the English rule, they would repair the roofs; the hospitals had proper medicines and doctors. The roads in the tea estate were clean and wide. The ponds would have clean water with myriad of water lilies and pink and red lotuses blooming in them. Water birds like cormorants and herons would nest there and storks would walk on their long wobbly legs on the small paths between the rice fields. At night, they would hear the deer call.

The rain had softened to a soft patter. Phoolbasiya had gathered in one corner all her belongings including the utensils. The hut was in imminent danger of coming down. A few days ago, there was a terrible storm that had lasted a few days. In the village someone had died after being struck with lightning. He had gone to get his cow grazing in the field. Poor thing! So many people became homeless after their roofs went flying through the sky. Khepli's hut came down as did that old banyan tree, its roots exposed to the elements. However, Phoolbasiya's ramshackle hut remained standing. It was a wonder how it withstood that storm. The storm had passed, and there was no more rolling of thunder. Phoolbasiya was scared of the thunder: who knew where the lightning would strike and who would die! It was scary even inside the hut. That year, Kala Mian had gone out to ply his rickshaw; his wife and two kids were inside the hut when lightning struck. All three had died. What games were those children playing while Kala Mian's wife cooked rice? In Makrichora, the thunder had been just as loud. Phoolbasiya used to wrap her arms around her grandmother when she heard the sound of thunder. '*Dadi*? Tell me a *khisa*, a story,' she would beg.

Dadi had died and she had not got to know about it. She used to love Phoolbasiya. She would often accompany her to forage in the forest in search of wild lemon or brinjals. Sometimes they dug in the soil for wild potatoes or hunted for banana flowers. One had to dig deep to find them. Here too, Phoolbasiya had often foraged in the forest to search for vegetables or herbs or dry sticks to light a fire. Her man used to work at the tea estate, feeding leaves into the machine. Her man was Subol, who had fallen in love with her when he had gone to Makrichora tea garden. And Phoolbasiya too had spun like a top. Her marriage had been fixed with someone at Srimangal tea garden, who was the son of Lakkiram Bauri. If she had married there, then she would not have lost her kin: her parents, her grandmother, siblings—all would have remained!

She had married Subol before the country was divided into Hindustan and Pakistan and had left Makrichora. She had not known then that she would never go back to her family, ever! Her father's home would be lost forever! Phoolbasiya had wept copiously, wept and wept. At one time she had thought she would lose her mind. How could a human heart bear so much pain? She could not do her household chores, and the man by her side seemed a stranger.

The rain had stopped now. The frogs were croaking softly like an ululation. Phoolbasiya remembered that during her marriage ceremony, there were such festivities: the sounds of ululation, dancing and music. Her father had killed a huge goat and the meat was cooked with pumpkin. There were fights too, physical and verbal. How could a marriage be without fights? No, she would no longer keep awake; she would sleep and not think of the past. The flat wooden stool, that Subol used to sit on to eat, was her pillow. She would try and sleep a bit.

Subol used to feed leaves in the machine and one day the machine had taken his right arm. They had taken him to Labok hospital and he recovered but without an arm. He could no longer work at the machine. He became a caretaker at the drying shed, the *dhoopghar*, and Phoolbasiya went to work too. She picked tea leaves. She picked tons and tons of leaves. When she would go to weigh them, the manager would stare at her. Oh yes, she was beautiful! So many men had stared at her or sent her propositions but Phoolbasiya was oblivious to them. She had been reticent and withdrawn. When Rami sang while plucking tea leaves, Phoolbasiya too became sad:

> Oh, dear friend, what sorrows can I speak of?
> My beloved forgot me after going off to another land
> My tears fall and drench my print sari, oh friend…

She did not know why she felt as she did. She forgot to pluck the leaves at hand and just stared at the sky where a few lazy white clouds floated by. An oriole had called nearby; in her mind, Phoolbasiya was back at Makrichora. She used to think that the clouds too went travelling there, in the tea garden that she knew so well; and the bird often went to sit on her jamun tree. Only she, Phoolbasiya, was not able to go back! Nor could her kin come to her!

Why was the country partitioned? Who partitioned it? What was the gain of such a division? Phoolbasiya did not know the answers to these questions! But what about the enormous loss that she had suffered? She lost all her loved ones. Why was she not able to return to the land of her birth? That way was lost too.

She had heard of Nehru and had heard that someone had shot at Gandhiji. But what about her return to Makrichora garden? Why was that stopped? Who stopped it? Phoolbasiya did not know then and did not know now. When Hindustan and Pakistan came into being, so many people came to where she lived but no one had come from the tea gardens. The refugees were settled in the land that was a part of many tea estates but she did not find anyone she knew.

When the war happened in East Pakistan, there was another wave of people who filled all the school buildings nearby. Phoolbasiya had thought that her family would be among them. She had taken a neighbour, Samir, with her to go and look at all the schools in the hope that she would find someone! But she did not see a single face that she loved: not her parents, nor her brothers. Her grandmother must have died already. She did not find anyone from the Makrichora tea estate! There were many refugees who had come from tea estates but not from the one that was close to her heart! She had big hopes that she would find her loved ones but where were they? Did the Khan soldiers butcher them all?

She had heard that a lot of people had been killed and countless women had been raped. The house where she worked had a radio. She often listened in when it was on. That was the time when Subol died of cholera. So many others died too: Sumli and Kausalya, Sita's mother. Phoolbasiya had no children. She had lost a child even before it was born and she never conceived again.

Once she had asked a Union guy to find out about her family in Makrichora but he had said that the tea workers did not have a union over there so it would be difficult to find out about them. Earlier, the tea garden labourers did not have voting rights; Phoolbasiya voted now. She did not understand so many things: she did not know how to sign her name. Yet everyone made her the leader and she would preside over Durga *Pujo* meetings and keep general peace. She loved the Lalchora tea garden but she could never forget Makrichora. Had the way been open, she would never have felt that kind of a thirst to return. She often cursed those who had made it impossible for her to return...*Die die...may all your family die!*

The rain had started again. Who knew why it rained so much? It seemed the earth would be washed away in the rain water. She could hear the song again:

Chand the trader had made a raft of banana stems
I will float upstream too in such a boat,
To a city called Ujani Nagar…

As night came to an end, the hut sank in the mud. In all the thunder and storms, nothing had happened to it but that night it just sank in the mud. Everyone came out when it was light. Where was Phoolbasiya? *Kaha gelo Phoolbasiya*? Was she alive? Find her…

But Phoolbasiya was away in flight: what happiness, what freedom! She was aloft in the sky, floating with the white fluffy clouds! What happiness! Oh, far away she could see her beloved Makrichora: Yes, Makrichora tea garden in Sylhet. How short the distance was and she hadn't been able to cross it all her life! She had suffered because she could not cross that small space of land. She could see her jamun tree, standing tall with leafy branches. The leaves hid black juicy fruits all over the bough. Someone was singing:

They took away your kin
They took away your home
They gave you tears, all lifelong…

Translated by Debjani Sengupta

THERE GOES SRIMATI

When Jagat Bauri's daughter, Sridam's wife, Srimati, got off the packed bus at Aranyapur Battala, the only train from Badarpur towards Bhairabi had blown its horn and left. The cuckoo had sung its last song of the day. The red sun was setting behind the mountains. Long lines of herons were returning home. Srimati lifted her face to watch them. The usual pair of eyes at Battala bazar rested upon Srimati's flesh.

'Isn't that Srimati? Sridam's wife, Srimati, who was sent to jail for murdering a man. She looks better than ever. Almost unrecognizable!'

'Nowadays, jails provide a luxury life.'

Srimati crossed the Battala with her head down. She made her way to the fields. If she took the shortcut through them, she would reach home faster. Sridam knew that she was going to be released from Hailakandi jail; why didn't he come to take her home? Was he ill? A few cars rushed by on the highway, campaigning for the coming election. *Who will you vote for?*

Srimati stopped abruptly and watched the line of passing cars. The election was going to take place again.

The four walls of the prison had barred Srimati from understanding anything at all. Four years had passed, one by one!

The first year took her aged mother-in-law; Sridam had carried the news to her. That too three months later. Srimati had cried profusely. Why wouldn't she? Her mother-in-law had loved her dearly. Throughout the day, the old woman remained engrossed with her daily chores. Once, while digging potatoes in the jungle, she had slipped and had twisted her ankle. She was bed-ridden for one month. During that time, she never let Srimati leave her side.

'Srimati? Is that Srimati?'

After the tea leaves were accepted and the workers paid, her mother-in-law used to buy nuts from the Talapshal market for her. She would come home and sit on the courtyard with her legs splayed out.

'Your daughter-in-law is plucking fruits off the guava tree.'

'Don't you worry! She is just a little girl; everything will fall into place when she grows up.'

And Srimati used to climb the guava tree and sing a filmy song, swinging her legs in the air. It wasn't as if she was very old, was she? Ummm…when she was married off, she was in class three of Bharat master's Kamala Sundori Pathsala.

A swarm of returning herons fluttered away. Srimati looked up, startled.

On the second year, her father had died. Sudam *kaka* was the bearer of bad news and Srimati had cried even more profusely. Who else did the old man have, except her? From Sudam *kaka*, she got to know that her father had died without a doctor, alone in his solitary room.

Tears flooded her eyes again. So innocent and foolish, she was at that time! She had asked her father: 'Everyone is saying that I will get married, Father.'

'Yes. You can't go to school from tomorrow.'

'And what about the hunting and marble games that I play? I will not marry, Father.'

'Do you think I am sending you far away from me? Your new home will be nearby.'

Nearby? Marriage was nothing but a smear of sindur on one's forehead, wearing shiny saris and going far away with a stranger while tears blinded one's eyes.

'Whom am I getting married to?'

'He is called Sridam.'

Sridam? The one whose forehead was once split open with a stone thrown by Srimati herself! That person will become her husband? Oh!

The sun had set. However, some remnants of its reddish hue were mixed up with the visible darkness. It felt so good to be free. After so long, Srimati was finally returning home, the home she had single-handedly built with such loving care. Who knew how much it has changed! And the cow, Dholi… was she still there? Perhaps she has grown old. There was also a calf born on a Tuesday, so Srimati had named her Mangala. Perhaps she was full-grown too. And what about the *seuli* tree? During the autumn months, the ground beneath the tree would be strewn with white flowers. Srimati used to weave garlands with them. Her aged mother-in-law loved watching her. During *Pujo*, from the Goddess to the *asur* at her feet, all had to be adorned with Srimati's woven *seuli* garlands.

In the visible darkness of the dusk, some men, busily discussing the election, passed by Srimati. Did they recognize her? She recognised one of them: Sudam *kaka*'s brother-in-law who worked as a field labourer. Another one was her mother-in-law's friends' brother's son. *What was his name?* And another one was…a duck squawked nearby. *Who was it?* Srimati was startled. Sunk in her thoughts, Srimati had already reached the Supal lake without noticing. The right road led to Padma Lake. How she loved to eat the *padma tona*! She used to sit at the edge of the lake and gaze at the herons! After the rains, her father used to bring home fish. Ma used to keep those big *singi, magur* and *koi* alive in a clay vessel. Once her father had asked her to make *paturi* out of the small fish that he had caught. She hadn't known how to, so her father himself marinated the fish with salt, oil, turmeric powder and chilies and wrapped it in a banana leaf to cook.

Ma had eloped with Subhash *kaka* by that time. Srimati could barely remember her face. The only thing she remembered was that during the *poush* festival when everyone strolled from one house to another carrying the Tusu figurine, Ma too had sung along:

Oh dark girl!
Your name is known everywhere!
Inside the bungalow, you indulged in playful acts
You lured the Saheb
Aren't you ashamed?
The paan stains on your dark lips
Don't suit you
Aren't you ashamed?

Srimati had seen a woman in jail who resembled her mother. She was reserved and quiet and mentally impaired. Sometimes she would sob, throw away her food and at other times she would be happy, smiling and making paan. Srimati used to get one. Nobody knew where she got the paan and betel nuts from.

There was another madwoman who hailed from a well-to-do family. She was the daughter of Bijon Babu, a teacher in a school. One day, she went mad. People said that she had been possessed by a Goddess and they came swarming to Bijon Babu's house to get a glimpse of the Goddess Bishhari. Srimati too had accompanied her mother-in-law. The girl possessed by Bishhari announced that she could kill and then resurrect her little brother. The head police inspector stood there dazed and so were a courtyard full of people! And she had drowned her little brother to death. What superstitious belief people had! Srimati's heart ached for that girl, incarcerated in jail.

Another one was Sudhanyo Bakti from Lalachora tea estate. He had once offered his love to Srimati but she had paid him no attention—through all her heart and existence had run Sridam's smile. It would be a sin to think of another man and she had barred herself from communicating with Sudhanyo.

Sudhanyo was returning from the market after selling Lala's cow around 3 am in the morning because the trading of cows was conducted only at midnight.

There had been a burglary in the residence of the heroin dealer, Samiran. The police, desperate to catch a thief, had decided to make Sudhanyo the burglar. While narrating that incident to Srimati, Sudhanyo would turn pale.

'You know, I have an old, blind mother at home.'

'Is there anyone else?'

'No. No one else except a bamboo flute.'

Now, as Srimati was finally returning home, she felt a kind of an anguish for Sudhanyo. A terrible anguish!

A little sliver of the moon was visible on the sky. *What was today's date?* The moon was accompanied by a star. *Was it the evening star?* When the evening star rose above the litchi tree, Srimati would abruptly stop reading her tables to silently gaze at it. According to Bharat master, this same star becomes the morning star at dawn. The moonrise would be soon after. Her mother would cook rice and start her daily ritual of cursing Srimati's father. But she would turn a deaf ear to all of that to watch the moon. The moon alone. Under a similar moon, she was once returning home from Lala's Sri Krishna cinema hall with Sridam.

'Aren't you Sridam?'

'Hmm.'

'Who is it with you? Your wife?'

'Hmm.'

'Where have you been to?'

'To Lala's.'

'What for?'

'To watch a movie.'

'It seems you pamper your wife quite a lot.' Saying this, the man passed Srimati, almost devouring her with his eyes.

'Who is this man?'

'Bhotu. Bhotu Dam.'

'The dacoit Bhotu?'

'Hmm.'

'Oh my God.' Srimati clung to Sridam in fear. 'He frightens me.'

Why wouldn't she be frightened? At least eight to ten murder charges were attached to Bhotu. The police had tried to arrest him but he had escaped after a bullet fight.

Srimati came back to her senses and resumed watching the moon and the trees. A fox howled nearby. Startled, she stopped again. She looked towards the hillock where her friend Fulbashia lived. A dim light was visible. An eagerness to know Fulbashia's whereabouts heaved inside her.

Had she been married off somewhere? She was a good girl, so straightforward and brave. Quite brave. That time when their land was getting occupied, she alone… *Oh my dear God!* A snake hissed past Srimati.

Once on a solitary afternoon, when Srimati was returning after filling her pot from the waterfall, the sight of the *kharish* snake had chilled her spines and she had screamed. It was then that Bhotu appeared from nowhere. Did Bhotu come in the guise of the snake or was it the snake impersonating Bhotu? The water pot had tumbled down from Srimati's head.

Yes, another day Srimati was singing the *Sagar Bhasa* song and bathing in the stream. Two wild cocks were pecking on the ground under the *chalta* tree. Suddenly, Bhotu had appeared from nowhere. Out of fear, Srimati had stopped singing and began to shiver. She stayed in the water for so long.

When the last of the moonshine was washing Aranyapur's trees and bushes, the streets and Srimati's home and hearth, under the thatched roof over the flowery printed sheets, Sridam was crushing Srimati with his love. Drenched in Sridam's love, it was then that Srimati mentioned Bhotu.

Smiling and crushing her all the more, Sridam said, 'Why would you be afraid, don't you have a *dao* at home? A weapon?'

Raising her head from Sridam's chest, Srimati had looked at him with wondering eyes.

That day the golden oriole was singing since the morning. Srimati had cleaned her house and courtyard while listening to the song. Then she had bathed and dried her hair. The sun was ready to set by then. Suddenly she had remembered, *Oh no! I haven't prepared the tea and chapattis yet.*

Her mother-in-law and Sridam would return soon. So she had she gone inside to light the kitchen fire and started kneading the flour. Just then Bhotu had pounced on her from the back.

Her mother-in-law was away plucking tea leaves and Sridam was at Bilgaon. Crushed between the robust arms of Bhotu, Srimati had choked. She heard a whisper near her ears, 'I will wrap you in gold, Srimati.'

'Don't you have a dao at home?'

'A dao?'

'Yes, a dao.'

Pushing him aside, the 18-year-old Srimati had stood up. Lifting the shining *dao*, Srimati had brought it down on Bhotu's body in a frenzy. A pool of blood. Srimati stood quivering. At least she had protected her honour. That day, Jagat Bauri's daughter, Sridam's wife, had declared herself a victor. She remembered Sudam *kaka* saying, 'You slew a big shot dacoit; you deserve a prize!'

The prize led her to the police station, from the police station to the court, from the court to the jail and hence four years passed one by one.

Srimati reached home. There stood the arjun tree whose bark was sought by people from far-off places. The rope on which Srimati hung her clothes to dry was still there. Yes, this was her home. But why was it so dark here? Where was he? He must have gone to the bazar.

Today was market day at Katlichera. He knew Srimati would come. What harm would have fallen if he had skipped one of his haat days? There would be plenty of haat days to come.

'Is that you Srimati?'

'Yes, *Kaka*. Why is it so dark here?'

'Did you come all alone, dear?'

'Why is it so dark here, *Kaka*?'

'Come. Today you will spend the night at my place.'

'Why *Kaka*? Where is he?' Srimati went numb.

'Gone to his in-laws.'

'In-laws?'

Srimati's legs were starting to give up. She was striving to keep herself upright.

'Yes, he got married last *Baisakh* and the wife is with child, they say. So he has gone to pay a visit.' Sudam *kaka* failed to conceal his deep sigh.

A fox howled from somewhere. This time the cry did not startle Srimati.

'Come, dear, come. Sridam will be here by tomorrow morning.'

But Srimati did not stir.

'What happened? Come.'

'No *Kaka*. You go. I shall not come.'

'You won't come?'

'No.'

For whom did I commit such a crime and protect my honour? What honour? What fidelity? *Thook*. She spat out a large ball of saliva. Then she turned around. Would she go and see her father's place once? No…let it be. She again walked back through those moonlit streets but this time it was not Sridam's wife or Jagat Bauri's daughter. It was Srimati who was walking. Let her walk…

Translated by Aishwarya Banerjee and Debjani Sengupta

UPSTREAM

'You won't go to cast your vote this time?'

'No.'

'Fine. Don't.'

'How many times have you asked me this question?'

'Thrice, I guess.'

'No dear, ten times already.'

'What's the reason you won't vote?'

'The reason is, I don't like any of the candidates.'

'Aren't you a citizen of this country?'

'Who said so?'

Mandakini's eyes were fixed on a branch of the *krishnachura* tree as she prepared breakfast.

'Look, what a lovely bird! Rubbing its beak on the branch.'

'What is its name?'

'I don't know.'

'It's neither a mynah nor a green pigeon, *nah*? It has a black body full of yellow patches with a yellow and scarlet beak. Beautiful!'

'I think I need to read Salim Ali,' Paramesh said, laughing. He lit a cigar, still grinning. Earlier, Mandakini used to forbid him from smoking too much. Now she said nothing.

At one time, Paramesh's drinking used to bewilder her. She had argued, cried. Now she did nothing, she was used to it. Life's another name was compromise. Compromise and then to go on living. No—Mandakini did not say anything to anyone anymore.

'Where are you, lost in thought? See, the unknown bird has flown away.'

Let it fly. After living forty years on this earth, did Mandakini recognize anyone? Suddenly, tears welled up in her eyes. Vehicles, carrying election campaign banners, rushed across noisily through the main road. This was indeed an easy time to buy divisive humanity cheap!

'Come, breakfast is ready.'

'Where's Mona?'

'She's off jogging.'

'When did she go out?'

'Early in the morning. She had asked me to make *dosa-sambar*. "I don't like the same old *luchi-dum aloo* that is your staple, Ma."'

'Look, our daughter is growing up. Don't admonish her.'

'What does that mean...'

'You won't eat?'

'No, I will wait for Mona.'

'Where is today's paper?' Paramesh plunged into the news while dipping a piece of *dosa* in the *sambar*. 'Look, what have they written in the papers!'

Mandakini did not listen or respond. Her eyes were fixed on the window, searching for the unknown bird...

Once, in the branches of Kali-than's peepal tree, a bird had given birth to many nestlings. She no longer remembered who had told her about them. But at dusk, Mandakini had arrived, holding baby birds wrapped in the hem of her dress.

'What is there in your palm?' Her grandmother had been shocked, as she lit the evening lamp for worship.

'Baby birds.'

'Birds? Where on earth did you get them?'

'Near the Kali temple.'

'O God, what did you do? Go, keep them back.'

'No.'

'Won't their mother cry?'

Mandakini had stared blankly, taken aback.

Wiping her tears, she had gone back to the tree with her grandmother and a torch to keep the nestlings back. It was dark then, and the moon had already risen.

'Look, at this news report.'

'What?'

'There is a conference of sex workers.'

Does a change of name also change the profession?

No one addressed how undignified the work was, neither was anyone concerned about rehabilitation, instead all were busy getting a name or some recognition. 'I don't like this Paramesh—it's like a conspiracy…'

'When everyone says…'

'Not everyone but many. One day, robbers and thieves will also seek acknowledgement.'

'How?'

'The legal right to loot. Just change the name, don't call them thieves.' Mandakini licked her dry lips.

Paramesh had completed his meal. He was still at the table, reading the newspaper. Mandakini walked past as she untangled her braided hair, tied up from the night before.

'Listen, Mandakini.'

'Yes?' Mandakini looked back.

'I won't have lunch today at home.'

'But I am cooking chilli chicken.'

'I have a lot of work today. I won't be able to leave office before evening.'

'On a Sunday?'

Her hair was untangled now and lay across her back. Mandakini looked at the *krishnachura* tree. The bird did not come back. Spring was over. Still the cuckoo sang *kuhoo kuhoo*.

'This chilli chicken tastes great, Mummy,' Mona remarked while having lunch.

'I think I have taught you to call me Ma, Mona.'

Mandakini was spreading the rice on her plate with her fingers.

'You are still so old-fashioned. Susmita's mummy...'

'Eat your food, Mona.'

'I wanted to talk to you.'

'Yes?' Mandakini was intent on her plate of rice.

'Do you know a beauty contest is taking place here?'

'No. I don't really keep myself informed of all this nonsense.'

'I will participate in the contest.'

'Don't.'

Mona took a big bite into the piece of chicken. 'Why not?'

'That's a conspiracy of capitalism.'

'You find a conspiracy in everything, Mummy.'

'Don't you see how women's bodies are used in advertisements? Film stars like Sushmita Sen and...'

'So what?'

'This country is like a big marketplace and Indian women are being made to win beauty pageants.'

Mona got up to leave. Her lunch remained on her plate, unfinished. Mandakini sat still. Loud music, coming from Mona's room, filled up the house. Mandakini was still searching for the unknown bird in the branches of the tree…

'What took you so long?'

'I just got back from office.'

'Will you have some tea?'

'Sure. Where's Mona?'

'At her dance class.'

The phone rang. As Mandakini picked up the receiver, someone disconnected the line on the other side.

'Who was that?'

'I don't know. It got disconnected. You know, Mona is very annoyed today,' Mandakini said as she handed over the tea cup to Paramesh.

'Why?'

'She wants to take part in a beauty contest.'

'Let her.'

'What do you mean?'

'I mean what's the issue if she goes?'

'You know I don't like all this. And you know this is a capitalist conspiracy to demean women...'

'Listen, going with the flow is the most intelligent thing to do nowadays. One can reach one's goal.'

'I don't know, Paramesh. Not everyone's goal is the same. And if the flow of the stream is filled with sludge, will you still allow yourself to go with that? Your own daughter?'

Paramesh said nothing.

Mandakini suddenly started to cry.

'You used to argue the same way at the University canteen with me. I never got annoyed.'

'No. Although we are together now, our thoughts and ideals are poles apart, Paramesh.' Mandakini left.

The moon was shining in the night sky outside. The trees were silent, deep in slumber. In the moonlight, Mandakini again searched for the unknown bird.

It had been raining continuously since yesterday morning. The Barak River was in full spate. The two banks of the river were overflowing. Water had gushed into the lanes and by-lanes of the small town of Silchar. No one sang the happy songs of monsoon in town. Monsoon brought only dread and worries. The election season was round the corner. According to the reports of the exit polls, this time Assam would see a change of party in governance and power. With so much hope and dreams, the masses changed the government but their dreams remained unfulfilled. Voters tried again and again. But no matter how many times they changed, the water in the glass remained muddy. *When would pure water fill the glasses of the people?* Mandakini became unmindful of her tasks as she cooked.

'I can't find my blue tie.'

'Why? It was in the closet only.' Mandakini came running from the kitchen. 'Here it is.'

Paramesh extends his hand.

'Why do you start yelling even before you look for it?'

Mona was also searching for something.

'What is it?'

'I can't find my pen. I am getting late for college.'

'Which one?'

'The pen I got on my birthday.'

'Here it is. Why don't you keep things in their place?'

Mandakini returned to the kitchen, running. Oh, the *halwa* had burnt. Paramesh liked it, that's why she was making carrot *halwa* with so much care. The maid was on leave; she had gone home to her village. So much work had piled up.

'Mummy?'

'What is it?'

'May I ask something? Will you make some meat fritters today?'

'Yes, I will,' smiled Mandakini.

Paramesh and Mona left as the rain continued. Raw guavas were peeping among the green leaves. The jasmine was in full bloom. A drenched crow was sitting on the branch of the areca nut tree. Mandakini started to search for that unknown bird in the rain drenched sky…

Today, after a long time, Mandakini sat down to play her *esraj*. Her favourite Raga Bihaag. The rain had stopped. The moon was visible from the window.

The phone was ringing.

'Hello?'

'Listen, I will be late today.'

'Mona has not returned yet.'

'What's the time?'

'Half past nine.'

'Wait for another half an hour. I will be home by then.'

The calling bell rang as soon as she put down the phone receiver.

Mona entered hurriedly.

'Sorry, I am late.'

'Wait. Where were you?'

'There was a function in college.'

'You could have told me.'

'Sorry, Mummy.'

'Go and freshen up.'

'No, I need to talk to you.'

'Go and have a wash. We can talk later.'

'No—listen to me first.'

'Let me bring the meat fritters and we can talk and eat.'

'There's a problem, you know,' Mona says, as she sits down on the sofa.

'Problem?'

'Yes. A little problem. I am pregnant, Mummy.'

The casserole filled with meat fritters fell off Mandakini's hands. No, not Mother Mary's face. Her friend Paromita's face flashed in front of her eyes; Paromita, who had killed herself. She could also see her long lost roommate Bishakha's face. Her aunt's face who had been ostracised by society for her daughter, Nandita.

'What did you say?' Mandakini struggled to breathe.

'I said I am pregnant. Why are you so worried?'

Mandakini felt a great urge to drive Mona out of the room. She thought of bludgeoning her to death. Somehow, she composed herself.

'Who is the father?'

'What?'

'Whom you are in love with.'

'In love? We had an affair. What will you do with him?'

'I will speak to him and his parents.'

'About what?'

'About the marriage.'

Mona laughed heartily.

Could someone laugh so heartily in such a situation? Mandakini felt dizzy with rage.

'I won't be able to marry that guy. He is my classmate. He writes poems. He has no career, Mummy.'

'Mona?' Mandakini was about to collapse. Yet she managed to stand straight.

'I was going to tell you about the abortion. Susmita said it can be done but without asking you...'

Mandakini withdrew her hand that was about to land on Mona's cheek. The phone was ringing. Let it ring. She looked at the sky outside. A wide stream was sweeping away her home. The one that she had made with all her dreams and struggles. The moon was playing hide and seek beneath the clouds. Mandakini wept for a long time. In the dull moonlight, among the rain-washed trees, she searched for that unknown bird, again.

As she was about to put in the wax gourd slices in hot oil, Mandakini stopped. What was the commotion at this early hour? All the while, Mandakini had tried to forget last night by listening to the cuckoo sing. Mandakini did not sleep for the entire night. Mona had gone jogging after waking up at dawn. Mandakini was about to say, *jogging at this time…* but she swallowed the words with great difficulty. Paramesh was very late last night. He was still not awake. Mandakini knew that he was having an affair with his colleague Sunayna, who was divorced. Hiding her sigh, Mandakini looked outside.

'Although I don't have money like you people, we have dignity, understand?' Shyamrati's daughter, Sanaka, landed a tight slap on the face of Agni Babu's son. 'You have the audacity to offer me illicit relations!' Shyamrati was yelling too.

Mandakini stopped listening. The wok was burnt red. But her heart leapt with joy after many days. Her weary, tired mind bloomed with the fragrance of lotus buds. Mandakini smiled as she stirred the wax gourd slices in the oil. She felt the urge to hug Sanaka, to touch her a little. Executive Paramesh's wife, brilliant student Monalisa's mother, a dignified homemaker—Mandakini—was feeling jealous of Sanaka's mother, Shyamrati, a brick kiln worker.

As she covered the wok with a lid, Mandakini looked outside. Oh, there was the unknown bird on the *krishnachura* branch! Mandakini climbed the stairs to go downstairs.

Her feet were sinking into the carpet of Australian grass in the garden. The bird was now at the jasmine bush. Then it flew away to the eucalyptus tree by the road. Oh, where did all this water come from? Mandakini was now running over the stream. Her legs were losing their balance as she ran against the flow. Yet she kept running. Let her run…

Translated by Shubha Mitra

GLOSSARY

DECEIT BROUGHT US TO ASSAM

Amabashya: Day of the new moon.

Hadiya: A rice-based fermented drink.

Jagran: An all-night festival of songs and dance for a Hindu deity.

Kaala Pani: The Cellular Jail in the Andaman and Nicobar Islands, a British colonial prison.

Kaalpurush: Stars in the Orion constellation that appear as the body of a man/hunter.

Kadai: An Indian wok-like utensil.

Kamini: A fragrant flowering creeper.

Karamer Dal: The Karam festival is a harvest festival where groups of young men and women dance and sing together.

Madol: A type of drum.

Mon: Maund, unit of weight.

Muluk: Country or kingdom.

Saat Bon Kritika: The star cluster known as Pleiades.

Seuli: Night-blooming jasmine.

SALUK FLOWERS HAVE BLOOMED

Anganwadi: A rural child care center in India.

Asha: Accredited Social Health Activists are community health workers especially in rural areas.

Babubhaji: A leafy vegetable.

Bhatarkhagi: A swear word directed at women that literally means someone who devours her husbands.

Chaitra: A Hindu calendar month from mid-March to mid-April.

Fara: Culms or the hollow stem of the bamboo.

Gandharaj: Gardenia.

Gorui: A common fish.

Harsingar: Another name for *seuli*.

Indira Awaas: The flagship housing programme for the rural poor started by the Indian Prime Minister Indira Gandhi.

Kochusaag: Taro leaf.

Muri: Puffed rice.

Nayantara: Indian periwinkle.

Pon: Pound, unit of weight.

Powa: Unit of weight, approximately 233 grams.

Saluk: Water lily.

Sirish: A tree native to the Indian subcontinent.

SANDHYAMANI, ANCHU BURA AND...

Birangona; A brave warrior woman. Often used in the context of the Liberation war in Bangladesh.

Bulbuli: Red-vented songbirds common in the region.

Chaghar: A large barn where tea leaves are dried and stored.

Chalta: Elephant apple.

Dahuk: White-breasted waterhen.

Dheki: Fiddle-head fern.

Fultusi: Plum-headed parakeet.

Helencha: Buffalo spinach.

Ishti kutum: Black-hooded oriole.

Jhumur songs: Also known as Jhumair, these are songs common among the indigenous people of the Chota Nagpur plateau like Jharkhand, Southwestern regions of West Bengal and Northern Orissa. In the Assam tea gardens, the presence of Jhumur songs indicate the migration of people from these regions.

Khana's maxims: Khana's *bachan* or proverbs are a part of folk literature in West Bengal and Bangladesh, directed at the rural agricultural life of the community.

Nachghar: Dance hall.

Phunkni: Blowpipe.

Pujo: A festival dedicated to the Goddess Durga.

Titir: Common quail.

THE BOY

Asur: A demon.

Dhoopghar: A large shed where tea leaves are dried; same as *chaghar*.

Jarul: A deciduous tree with bright pink or purple flowers called crepe myrtle.

THE WITCH

Begun: Aubergine.

Bigha: Land measurement.

Chamar: A Dalit caste group, traditionally associated with leather works.

Dhai: Midwife.

Jatra: Folk performances; mostly on mythological or social narratives.

Jhinge: Ridge gourd.

Kajallata: A kind of vegetable.

Kavach: A pendant that acts as a protection against evil eye.

Lau: Gourd.

Siliker: Made of silk.

Tabiz: A locket.

ENCEINTE WOODLANDS

Cham: Rose apple.

Shravana: Monsoon month in the Hindu calendar from late July to late August.

Thakur dalan: A partly open courtyard where the idol of a God is placed.

SISIRKONA WILL PLAY ON

Aalaap: An improvised prelude to an Indian raga.

Bhairavi: A raga, associated with Lord Shiva, is sung in the morning.

Dhamar: A taal with 14 beats, grouped asymmetrically.

Keherwa: An eight beat taal of Hindustani music.

Mizrab: A plectrum used to play stringed instruments like the sitar.

Ostad: Maestro; a guru who teaches a disciple a form of the performing arts.

OOZING

Machan: An elevated platform made of bamboo and straw.

Pitha: Rice flour sweetmeats stuffed with coconut and jaggery.

Tusu: Tusu, known as Tusu *parab*, is a harvest festival celebrated in winter by the Adivasi communities in the eastern part of India. The festival includes community singing and dancing with special prayers to the Goddess Tusu who is both a cosmic deity and a child. A clay figurine is carried from home to home and worshipped.

TROUBLED TALES

Baganiya: Labourers who worked and lived inside tea gardens. They originated from the different provinces but once inside, their regional/tribal/caste identities were erased and they just became 'baganiya.' Even their mother tongues became a hybrid of many languages.

Baisakh: In the Hindu calendar, *Baisakh* is the onset of summer, starting from mid-April to mid-May, marking the Bengali new year.

Dolu bamboo: A special species of bamboo, evergreen and perennial with short rhizomes.

Jitiya: A Hindu festival common in Bihar, Jharkhand and Nepal, undertaken by women who fast to ask for their children's long life.

Kamranga: Star fruit.

Kauya: A red coloured fruit that grows in jungles.

Khatiya: A string bed.

Morod: Man; also denoting husband.

Paan: Betel leaf.

PHOOLBASIYA BURI GOES BACK

Beel: Lake.

Bhagat: God man; a saint.

Cham kathal: A type of jackfruit.

Chand Saudagar, Behula, Lakkhindar: Behula sailed with the dead body of her husband Lakkhindar who died on their wedding night after a snake bite. His father, Chand Saudagar, refused to worship the Goddess Manasa who sent a snake to kill Lakkhindar on his wedding night.

Goddess Manasa: Revered in rural areas of Eastern India who reigns over snakes.

Laishabi songs: Songs of the Manipuri tribes.

Mukhjhuta: Rice eating ceremony when the child is given solid food for the first time.

THERE GOES SRIMATI

Chalta: Elephant apple.

Dao: A machete.

Goddess Bishhari: Manasa, the Goddess of snakes.

Haat: A weekly village market.

Kharish: A cobra.

Padma tona: Juice of the lotus.

Pathsala: A village school.

Paturi: Fish cooked in mustard sauce, wrapped in banana leaves and steamed or roasted.

Poush: Winter months in Hindu calendar.

Sagar bhasa song: Songs sung in the folk theatre (jatra) titled Sagar Bhasa.

Singi, magur: Common varieties of fish.

GLOSSARY

UPSTREAM

Dosa: A South Indian crepe made from rice batter.

Esraj: A musical instrument.

Halwa: An Indian confection.

Krishnachura: a deciduous tree with bright red-orange flowers, also known as the flame tree.

Luchi: Fried bread made of all-purpose flour.

Raga Bihaag: A Hindustani classical raga.

Sambar: A South Indian stew made with lentils and vegetables.

KIINSHIP TERMS

Baba: Father.

Bou: Bride, often used as an address.

Buri: Old woman.

Buro/ Bura: Old man, often used as an address.

Dada: Older brother.

Dadu: Grandfather

Didi: Older sister.

Kaka: Uncle; literally, paternal uncle.

Kaki: Aunt; a common title given to older women.

Mashi: Maternal aunt.

Pisha: Paternal uncle, husband of Pishi.

Pishi: Aunt; literally, paternal aunt.

A NOTE ON THE VARIOUS SONGS

The *baganiya* people often put together songs celebrating their lives that featured Krishna/Shyam and Radha (his consort), two figures from the Hindu mythology. The figures epitomised a relationship of love and tenderness.

EDITOR'S ACKNOWLEDGEMENT

I was introduced to Jhumur Panday's short story collection *Sukh Gacher Golpo* many years ago by a friend, Professor Nandita Basu, who taught at the Department of Modern Indian Languages at Delhi University. Subsequently over the years, I included some of Jhumur's stories in translation for three anthologies that I co-edited. So, a grateful thanks goes to Nandita, voracious reader and an admirer of all things literary, for turning my attention to an important voice from the Barak Valley.

This book would not have seen the light of the day without the enthusiasm and engagement of Jhumur Panday. I met her for the first time in March 2024 and felt an instant connection with her disarming warmth and quiet intellect. When she suggested that I edit an English collection of her stories, I agreed without any reservation. It was a propitious time to get these stories out in the world to an even wider audience, especially when our common humanity was increasingly under question. Thank you, Jhumur, for being who you are and for lighting up our world with your words.

My grateful thanks to Nirmal Kanti Bhattacharjee of Niyogi Books for his unstinting support for this venture. Right from the book's genesis and through its execution, he was always ready with advice and encouragement and I benefitted vastly from them. This volume owes him much.

Warm thanks to Shirsha Ghosh who brought her own enthusiasm to the editing table and went through the manuscript with such patience.

I must applaud Pinaki De for a cover that is true to the stories and to the values they uphold.

My grateful thanks to all the translators whose words have enabled these stories to catch flight: Aishwarya Bannerjee, Kallol Choudhury, Mohan L. Zaigirdar and Shubha Mitra.

This book is dedicated to the people of Barak Valley whose language, history and very identity is deeply enmeshed with their land. I met many good people on my travels there and it may be impossible to name all of them but my grateful thanks to Sabyasachi Roy and Monolina Nandi Roy of Karimganj College for sharing their deep knowledge of Barak Valley's history with me. My warmest thanks to Professor Deepak Kumar Nair of Silchar, who introduced me to the intricacies of Sylheti language and the history of the tea gardens. I will be forever grateful for our road trip to Hailakandi!

A grateful thanks to Nirjhor Kanti Pal of Karimgunj, who epitomised the hospitality and warmth of Barak Valley's people.

Thank you, Avishek Ray, for being a companion par excellence on our travels to Karimganj and to a forgotten monument of 1857 at Malegarh.

My sister, Nandini Chatterjee (1967-2025), would have been very happy to hold this book in her hands. No words can possibly express how much we miss her!

Debjani Sengupta
April, 2025